Willie to the Rescue

To Allison:
Have fun with
"Willie!"
John SD'Amica

Books in the

STABLE SERIES

Book 1
Lady's Big Surprise
Hardback ISBN-13: 978-0-9746561-5-1
Paperback ISBN-13: 978-0-9746561-6-8

Book 2
Star of Wonder
Hardback ISBN-13: 978-0-9746561-3-7
Paperback ISBN-13: 978-0-9746561-4-4

Book 3
Willie to the Rescue
Hardback ISBN-13: 978-0-9746561-0-6
Paperback ISBN-13: 978-0-9746561-2-0

Book 4
Mary and Jody in the Movies
Hardback ISBN-13: 978-0-9746561-1-3
Paperback ISBN-13: 978-0-9746561-9-9

Praise for the
Lucky Foot Stable Series

"Dawson's experience as an educator and director of an Equine Institute serve her well in these novels. These exciting books will enthrall eight-to-twelve-year-old girls."

~Troy Michelle Reinhardt,
ForeWord Magazine

"Anyone who enjoys a great tale of horses and youth will find this a fascinating read. This most entertaining story moves swiftly in a non-preaching way while dealing with some very real issues... peer pressure, decision making, responsibility, self-esteem and learning to care about others."

~ Ellie Mencer,
Lockhouse to Lighthouse Magazine

Lucky **3** Foot

BOOK 3 in THE LUCKY FOOT STABLE SERIES

Willie to the Rescue

JoAnn S. Dawson

Willie to the Rescue: Book 3 in the Lucky Foot Stable series
by JoAnn S. Dawson

Published by F. T. Richards Publishing — www.luckyfootseries.com.
Available to the trade from Biblio Distribution, Inc. Contact them at
800-462-6420 or visit www.bibliodistribution.com.

Cover and interior illustration by Michelle Keenan
Lucky Foot Stable illustration by Tim Jackson
Cover and interior design by Pneuma Books, LLC
For more information, visit www.pneumabooks.com

Printed and bound in the United States of America
11 10 09 08 07 06   6 5 4 3 2 1

Publisher's Cataloging-in-Publication Data
(Prepared by The Donohue Group, Inc.)

Dawson, JoAnn S.
   Willie to the rescue / JoAnn S. Dawson.
     p. : ill. ; cm. -- (Lucky Foot Stable series ; Book 3)
   Hardcover ISBN-13: 978-0-9746561-0-6
   Hardcover ISBN-10:0-9746561-0-0
   Softcover ISBN-13: 978-0-9746561-2-0
   Softcover ISBN-10: 0-9746561-2-7
1. Horses--Juvenile fiction. 2. Friendship--Juvenile fiction. 3.
Horses--Fiction. 4. Best friends--Fiction. 5. Mystery fiction. I.
Title.

PS3554.A97 W55 2005
813.6   LCCN: 2005933558

To Mom and Daddy,
for raising me with horses

Lucky Foot Stable

Table of Contents

Table of Contents

1
Intruders on the Farm

CHANGES WERE COMING to the McMurray dairy farm, and Willie was not the least bit happy about it. Mr. McMurray had decided to expand his herd of Holstein milking cows, and that expansion would require the addition of a new farm hand — not to take the place of Willie, of course, after thirty years of loyal service, but to help in the daily workload typical of a busy dairy. Mr. McMurray had broken the news to Willie the day before, explaining that it was for the best, and that now Willie could take some time off. But the old farm hand wanted none of it.

He had just finished the afternoon milking and was hobbling past the open doors of Lucky Foot Stable when Mary and Jody burst into the sunshine to garner his advice on their latest crisis.

"Willie! We're trying to get Star to square up like you showed us, but he won't do it! He won't even try!" Jody cried.

"He keeps stomping his foot and snorting at us!" Mary added.

Mary and Jody had been working for months to prepare the cantankerous colt for a yearling halter show in a nearby county, and Willie had been their guide. But this morning, he was in no mood for their problems.

"Daggonit, can you two ever pass a day without buggin' me about somethin'?" Willie growled, never slowing his pace. "I got problems of my own to worry about!"

Mary and Jody stood in stunned silence, staring at Willie's back as he continued up the gravel path toward the little tenant house where he lived on the farm. They knew Willie could be grumpy at times, even as cantankerous as the colt they were trying to train, but they had never heard such an edge in his voice.

Without a word the girls turned and walked back through the stable doors. Mary sat on a bale of hay and Jody picked up a broom and swept a few wayward pieces of straw from the dirt floor.

"I wonder what's wrong with Willie?" Mary finally asked.

"I don't know, but I guess we should leave him alone for a while," Jody answered quietly.

"But we *can't* leave him alone!" Mary cried, jumping up from her bale and pacing back and forth in agitation. "He's *got* to help us with Star! The show is only two months away!"

"Well, Willie's already shown us most of the things we need to work on," Jody continued, "so maybe we can do it ourselves."

Mary looked at Jody in disbelief. "Do it ourselves? Jody, the way Star is acting up, I'm beginning to wonder if we can do it even with Willie helping us!" Mary stopped pacing and looked out the door into the paddock. "I mean, come look at him right now!"

Jody threw down her broom and joined Mary at the Dutch door of the stable. She spotted Star in the far corner of the paddock by the loading ramp.

"Oh my gosh!" Jody exclaimed.

Finnegan, the cow herding dog, was at the top of the loading ramp. Mary and Jody, in their haste to run from the stable and appeal to Willie, had left Jody's crop in the paddock, and Star had quickly adopted it as his new toy. The handle of the crop was now in Star's mouth, and the other end was in Finnegan's. The girls watched in amazement as colt and dog played tug of war with the crop, Finnegan growling and Star shaking his head from side to side in an attempt to loosen Finnegan's grip. Finally the colt wrenched the crop from Finnegan's teeth, threw his head up, and took a victory gallop around the paddock, kicking and bucking and waving the crop for joy.

Mary and Jody looked at each other in dismay, and without a word they turned from the paddock to contemplate what to do next. Before they could even begin their brainstorming, Finnegan began barking furiously. The girls, figuring he was barking at Star's antics, didn't even look up until they heard the noise out on the gravel lane.

Peering out from the back door of Lucky Foot Stable, Mary and Jody were astonished at what they saw. A rickety old blue flatbed pickup truck with deep dents marking the passenger side door rattled past, backfiring as it went. The girls had seen trucks come and go before, but never one quite as curious as this. For on the bed of the truck, piled high and tied with baling twine and rough rope, was what seemed to be a complete collection of someone's earthly possessions. Beds, chairs,

An ancient blue flatbed pickup with deep
dents rattled past, backfiring as it went.

a refrigerator, a washing machine, blankets, pillows, lamps, and tables were all piled helter-skelter. And the crowning glory, a huge white rabbit in a cage, was strapped to the very top of the mound. As the truck rumbled by, the girls caught a glimpse of the passengers, who were all crammed into the cab like sardines, no telling just how many.

"What in the…" Mary's voice trailed off. The truck came to a stop by the old house trailer that sat next to Mr. McMurray's tractor shed, and Mary and Jody watched with mouths agape as the driver's side door creaked open and passengers began emerging. Finnegan crouched on the ground next to the girls, sniffing the air and growling low in his throat.

"We've got to get Willie!" Jody whispered, grabbing Mary by the arm. "I think these people are trespassing or something! Come on, Finney!"

The girls took off at a gallop toward Willie's tenant house with Finnegan close behind. They were just about to jump onto the porch when Willie appeared in the doorway.

"What in tarnation…" Willie began.

"Willie!" Mary yelled. "You've got to come on the double! Some people just pulled up to the house trailer in an old pickup truck with all kinds of stuff tied on it, and they're getting out of the truck like they're about to move in or something!"

Willie's face looked like a thundercloud as he absorbed this information, then he shook his head and pulled on his earlobe. "Well," he said, squinting up at the sun, "I reckon they look like they're about to move in because they *are* about to move in. I just didn't think it would be this soon."

"What do you mean, Willie?" Jody cried. "Why would people be moving into the house trailer?"

"Because I'm gettin' old, that's why. Any more questions?" Willie answered in the same harsh voice he had used earlier. Then he took off his farm cap, slapped it against his knee, said "come on, dog," and went back inside the tenant house with Finnegan, slamming the door behind him.

For the second time that day Mary and Jody could only look at each other. Then they turned and flew up the gravel drive to the big stone house where Mr. and Mrs. McMurray lived. Not even stopping to catch their breath, they took turns knocking furiously on the double front doors. Before very long, the doors were pulled open and Mrs. Mc-Murray stood in the center, a doorknob in each hand.

"What's all this, then?" Mrs. McMurray asked in her lilting Irish brogue. Surprised by the panicked look on the faces of the two girls, she continued, "whatever is wrong?"

"Oh, Mrs. McMurray, we don't know what's wrong," Jody said, red-faced and pant-ing. "But there are some people down by the old house trailer, and… and… "

" …and Willie's mad about it, and we

don't know why, and he just slammed the door right in our faces!" Mary finished.

Mrs. McMurray brushed a strand of silver hair from her face and wiped her hands on her apron. She gazed down the lane at the little tenant house where Willie lived and then at the distraught girls waiting expectantly for an answer. Saying nothing, she turned and beckoned for Mary and Jody to follow her into the house.

"Would you girls like a cup of tea?" Mrs. McMurray asked with a polite smile. Mary and Jody sat side by side at the wooden trestle table in the middle of the blue and yellow farm kitchen, wriggling impatiently while Mrs. McMurray took two delicate china cups from the corner cabinet.

"Oh yes, ma'am, we're really thirsty," Mary answered for both of them. Mrs. McMurray placed the cups on the oilcloth table cover and carefully poured hot tea from a kettle into each cup. When she turned her back to replace the kettle on the stove, Mary and Jody made faces at each other. They had expected iced tea!

"Now, girls," she said, turning from the stove and crossing her arms, "I think you know that Willie's getting on in years."

Mary and Jody looked puzzled.

"Why, he's been with us for more than thirty years, and with the horses for some twenty before that…"

At the word *horses* Mary and Jody raised their eyebrows with interest.

"So Mr. McMurray thought it would be a good idea, with us expanding the herd and all, for Willie to have some help."

The girls' mouths slowly dropped open but no sound came out as Mrs. McMurray's explanation gradually sunk in. The people down at the house trailer were moving onto the farm! Intruders on their domain! Taking Willie's place! It couldn't be true!

"Now, they're not taking Willie's place,"

Mrs. McMurray assured, as if reading their minds. "Just helping out, you know. But Willie's set in his ways, and I know he's not too happy about it."

Mary and Jody didn't speak but shook their heads in unison.

Mrs. McMurray sat down on the wooden bench across from the two girls and leaned in conspiratorially.

"I know Willie's been helping you with the baby," she murmured. Mrs. McMurray always called Star *the baby* even though he was more than a year old now. "So maybe if he keeps on with that and you two make sure he knows you need him, he'll be able to get used to the idea of being away from the cows sometimes. What do you think?"

The girls looked at each other and then at Mrs. McMurray. "Willie *has* been helping us with Star and with Lady and Gypsy too…" began Mary.

"Yes, ma'am — did you know that Willie helped us take Lady to the horse show and that he taught Gypsy to pull the sleigh?" Jody asked.

Before Mrs. McMurray could answer, Mary went on, "...but he's always so busy that as soon as we really get started with something, he has to quit and go for the milking..."

"...and there's a yearling show in June that we want to go to, but Star's not ready, and we don't think he'll ever be ready, he's so 'daggone ornery,' as Willie says. But if Willie had more time..." Jody finally stopped to take a breath, and Mrs. McMurray took the opportunity to get a word in.

"There you have it then. You girls will just have to convince Willie that he's got to help you more. Then maybe he won't miss the cows so much."

"We'll try, Mrs. McMurray. But I think Willie's so mad at us right now he won't listen to us at all," Mary sighed.

"It's not you he's mad at, Mary. He's mad at the way life moves on, and there's no stopping it." Mrs. McMurray gazed out the window, a faraway look in her eyes. But suddenly she slapped her palms down on the oilcloth, making the girls jump. "Now off you go, and do your best," she said cheerily. "I'll show you out…but… you girls haven't touched your tea!"

"Oh, that's OK, Mrs. McMurray, we weren't as thirsty as we thought. And don't worry, we'll take care of Willie," Mary promised, skipping down the hallway arm in arm with Jody. As they stepped out into the sunshine, Mary turned to face the kindly woman once more and asked, "Mrs. McMurray, what was it you said about Willie being 'with the horses' for twenty years? What did you mean?"

"Well, you'll just have to ask Willie about that," she replied with a wink.

2
Meeting Annie

MARY AND JODY decided not to bother Willie just then with their questions about the horses, even though they were about to burst, wanting to know all about it. Instead they walked back to Lucky Foot Stable, glancing curiously at the house trailer as they strolled by and trying to look nonchalant. Much to their dismay, no one was to be seen outside the trailer, and they were surprised to see that most of the household goods had already been unloaded from the rusty old pickup.

"Wow," whispered Mary, "they work fast! There must be a lot of them."

"Well, there can't be too many," Jody replied. "There isn't that much room in there."

"I guess we'll soon find out," Mary said, breaking into a trot. "I have an idea! Let's go bring Gypsy and Lady in from the pasture, and we'll go riding around the farm. Then we can keep an eye on what's going on over there without being too obvious."

"Mare! That's so sneaky…" Jody giggled, "…but it is a good idea!"

The girls laughed as they ran the last few yards to the stable. They checked on Star, who had settled down and was munching on his hay in the corner of the paddock, and grabbed two lead ropes, one for each pony. When they arrived at the cow pasture, they found Lady and Gypsy taking a break from grazing and standing head to tail under the weeping willow tree, lazily switching flies from the other's ears.

"Gypsy! Ladabucks!" Mary called. "Wake up! We are going to do some investigating!"

Lady's reaction to this grand announcement was a gaping yawn, and Gypsy immediately turned her back to Mary and dropped her head to graze.

"Gypsy Amber!" Mary insisted, clipping the lead rope onto the mare's halter. "We are going to the stable and getting your bridle on. Then we are going to ride around and check out the invasion of the new people on the farm."

"Invasion?" Jody giggled, leading Lady toward the gate. "You make it sound like they're aliens or something."

"Well, who knows? Maybe they are. We haven't seen them yet, have we?"

"No, but we have to give them a chance. They could be perfectly nice," Jody said generously.

"Could be. Now let's quit yappin', as

Willie would say, and get bridled up. Time's a-wastin'!"

The girls trotted the ponies the last few yards to the stable and led them inside to their stalls. Out of the tack trunks came brushes, hoof picks, and combs, and they went to work grooming the dusty ponies from head to hoof. Jody worked silently, concentrating on getting the tangles out of Lady's unruly black mane, while Mary whistled a tune. So busy were they, making sure all the dirt was removed from the ponies' coats, that they didn't notice the shadowy figure who appeared in the open back door of Lucky Foot Stable.

"I'll get the bridles!" Mary yelled, skipping to her tack trunk with brushes in hand. Then she screamed, "aaahhh!" and dropped every brush to the floor.

Startled, Jody came flying out of Lady's stall. "What happened?" she cried. Then she stopped and stared, openmouthed.

Standing still and silent in the open doorway of Lucky Foot Stable was a knock-kneed skinny little freckle-faced girl with bright red hair tied up in pigtails and brown-rimmed glasses perched on the end of her upturned nose. She wore cutoff green shorts, a red and white checked shirt, and no shoes. Mary and Jody looked at the girl and the girl looked back at them. Finally the girl broke the silence.

"Hi," she said.

"Hi," Mary and Jody replied in unison.

"Whatcha doin'?" the girl asked, squinting into the dimness of the stable.

Mary and Jody looked at each other. "Um, we're just grooming our ponies," Jody answered.

"Ponies? I love ponies. Can I see 'em?" the girl asked, walking right past Mary and Jody and over to Lady's stall. The two surprised girls stood with their hands on their hips and watched as the girl reached up and patted Lady's nose.

"She's pretty," she said

"What's your name?" asked Mary.

"My name is Annie. Annie Mooney. I live here now."

"My name is Annie. Annie Mooney. I live here now."

Mary and Jody responded to this matter-of-fact statement with silence. They watched as Annie Mooney went to Gypsy's stall. "Come here, girl. Are you a girl? Come on over here so I can pet you," she demanded. And Gypsy did come over, much to Mary's surprise. Usually, when there was hay in her stall, nothing distracted Gypsy from eating. But there she stood, hanging her head over the stall door and letting this stranger scratch behind her ears.

"What's her name?" Annie asked.

"Gypsy Amber. Gypsy for short," Mary replied, becoming a little annoyed at the obvious enjoyment Gypsy was displaying at the scratching of her ears. "Don't you want to know our names?"

"Oh, OK, sure I do," Annie replied, turning to Mary expectantly. "What are they?"

"I'm Mary, and this is Jody."

"Pleased to meet you," Annie said, shaking

Mary's hand first, and then Jody's. "Do you live here?" she asked.

"No," Jody replied. "We live down the road. My house is in one direction, and Mary's is in the other. But we're here every day after school, and the whole weekend," she added quickly, lest this new girl think she had the upper hand.

"Oh. Well, I guess I'll see you around, then." And with that, Annie Mooney turned on her heel and walked out of Lucky Foot Stable.

Mary and Jody said not a word, only stared at the open doorway. Finally, Jody picked up her broom and Mary slowly gathered up the brushes she had dropped in the aisle. Mary deposited the grooming tools in her tack trunk and then turned to face Jody.

"Well," she said.

"Hmphh," sniffed Jody.

Nothing more was said as Mary picked up the bridles and Jody finished sweeping the aisle. But in each of the girl's minds were troubling thoughts of the changes that would take place as these new people "invaded" the farm. Mary and Jody began to understand Willie's feelings on the matter. But for now, they kept their thoughts to themselves.

"Do you still feel like riding?" Jody asked Mary.

"Mmm, not really," Mary said. "I think we just found out at least part of what we wanted to know. Maybe we should try and work with Star some more."

Bridles were put back where they belonged in the tack trunks and Star was led in from the paddock. Mary sat on a bale of hay and watched while Jody crosstied him and groomed him half-heartedly. Then they led him back out to the paddock and went to work using the training methods Willie had shown them to get Star ready for the in-hand yearling class at the county horse show.

Jody led Star in a circle around the paddock while Mary acted as announcer.

"Walk, please, all walk. Please use half the ring only," Mary intoned solemnly. Star walked nicely around the "ring," only once pushing Jody on the back with his muzzle.

"Now trot, please, all trot," Mary continued. Jody slid her hand down the lead rope, giving Star a little more of his head, and quickened her own pace to a trot, hoping Star would follow. But as soon as he felt the tug on his halter, he planted his feet and pulled back, stomping his foot and snorting stubbornly.

"Come on, Star!" Jody cried, and pulled again. But Star was having none of it. This time he reared halfway up and came down with both front hooves planted even more firmly than before. Jody turned to face him and with both hands pulled on the lead rope with all her might. But the harder she pulled toward her, the harder Star pulled away.

"What is goin' on here?" a familiar voice asked from the open Dutch door of the stable. "Is that what I taught you to do?"

"Willie!" Jody exclaimed, happy to see the old cowhand, even if he was in a bad mood. "Star won't trot, no matter what I do!"

"Well, he ain't trottin' *because* of what you're doin'!" Willie said. "How many times do I have to tell you — you don't turn and face him like that and pull with both hands. The more you do that, the more he'll pull back."

"Well, what should we do, Willie?" Mary asked, almost forgetting not to use her announcer voice. "He has to be able to trot nicely around the ring for the show, and he just won't do it."

"Well, you shoulda waited for me to help you. Now he's in an ornery mood, and he won't want to do nothin' right. We'll have to try somethin' new today. Let me get my rope."

Mary and Jody looked at each other fearfully when Willie walked away to get "his rope." Although the cowhand had been nothing but gentle and patient with Star up until this point, the girls were afraid of what he might do considering the mood he was in, and he had never mentioned a rope before. Jody patted Star nervously on the neck until Willie came back with a long section of soft thick rope in his hands.

"Um, Willie," Mary said hesitantly, "you're...you're not going to hurt him, are you?"

Willie stopped in his tracks and furrowed his brow, giving Mary the sternest look she had ever seen on his face. "Hurt him? Have I ever hurt him before?" he asked, raising one eyebrow and waiting for a reply.

"Um, no," said Mary meekly, blushing and looking at her toes.

"Then I guess that means I ain't gonna hurt him now," Willie said. "But I might feel like hurtin' *somebody* if any more stupid questions get asked. Now, Jody, bring him over here."

Jody quickly did as she was told, knowing it wouldn't be a good idea to argue with Willie today. The girls watched silently as

Willie expertly handled the rope, making a large loop in one end. The loop was gently placed around Star's rump. His tail was in the middle, and the long section of the rope was brought up over his back. Then Willie threaded the end of the rope through Star's halter ring. Star calmed down and stood still in response to Willie's gentle hand. Mary and Jody stood hypnotized, watching him.

"Now I'm goin' to lead him by this rope, and when I lead him forward, the loop around his rump will push him a little at the same time."

Willie held the rope in his right hand and stood on Star's left, then he walked forward a step. Star started to follow as normal, but when he felt the unfamiliar rope pushing on his rump, he lurched forward in surprise, stopping to look at Willie as if to say, "What's all this?"

"That's all right, boy, you'll get used to it. Come on now." Willie took another step, and another and after the first few hops and starts, Star became accustomed to the rope and walked along as he always did.

"Now call for the trot, Mary. Use your best voice," Willie instructed.

"Trot, please, all trot," Mary announced grandly. Willie pulled a little more strongly on the front end of the rope and began to trot himself, and Star had no choice but to go along, as the rope pulled him in the front and pushed him from behind. In no time Star was trotting easily around the paddock, lifting his head prettily and almost looking like a show horse. After three turns around, Willie slowed him to a halt and patted him on the neck.

"Willie! He did it!" Jody exclaimed. "He almost looked like he was having a good time!"

Willie removed the rope from Star's hindquarters and wound it carefully in his hands. "That's enough for today," he said quietly. "Once they do what you want them to, you don't want to overdo it and make them tired of it. We'll work on it again this week."

Mary took this opportunity to bring up the subject Mrs. McMurray had impressed upon the girls concerning Willie. "Willie, speaking of working with Star — now that the new people are here, you'll have more time, right?"

Jody held her breath waiting for Willie's reply, but no reply came.

Mary continued, "We saw one of them, Willie. We met a girl. I don't think we like her."

Willie turned sharply to Mary and took off his hat. Then he looked at Jody and paused before he spoke, as if trying to find the right words.

"I met one of them too," he said quietly. "I met that girl's daddy on the way over here. He told me that her mama, his wife, passed away, and then he took sick and lost his farm. He's raisin' three kids on his own, and now he's got no choice but to work on somebody else's farm just to make ends meet."

Mary and Jody lowered their gaze to the ground, red-faced and ashamed of themselves for not giving Annie Mooney a chance.

"So don't be sayin' you don't like somebody before you know anything about them," Willie continued. "If you do, you'll be just the same as me." And without another word, he turned and walked out the gate of the paddock.

3
Loading Star

THE NEXT TWO MONTHS passed quickly. Mary and Jody worked with Star every day, and sometimes Willie helped them. Now the horse show was only a week away. The girls were a little nervous because, even though Star behaved himself most of the time, there were days when he just wouldn't do a thing they asked of him, even with Willie helping them.

"That's partly because he's just got a bad ornery streak and partly because you girls spoiled him to death when he was little,"

Willie explained. "There's nothin' to be done about it now, except to keep on with his trainin' and hope he grows out of it."

But Mary and Jody worried that Star would choose the day of the show as one of his bad days. He had never been off the farm before, and they had no idea what he would do once he arrived at the showgrounds. But the one thing they did have control over was teaching him to load onto the bed of Willie's pickup truck. And that was the training they focused on the Saturday afternoon exactly one week before the show.

"Jody, remember when we took Lady to that other horse show in Willie's truck and you were so embarrassed because we didn't have a trailer like everybody else?" Mary asked while Jody brought Star in from the paddock to get him ready for his loading lesson.

"Yes, I remember, and it's not going to be any better this time. I bet we'll still be the only ones there with a pony riding in the back of a pickup truck."

"Well, what are we going to do about it? We don't have a trailer, and the sides are already on the truck, ready to go. I just hope there will be a place to unload him at this show. We've never been there before."

Jody, busy picking Star's hooves, didn't reply. She finished that job and began combing his tail as Mary lazily sat on a bale of hay and leaned back against the front boards of Lady's stall. She almost fell asleep as she watched Jody work. Just as Mary's eyes were about to close, she was jolted awake by the sudden landing of a bird on her head.

"Walter!" she giggled. "I wondered where you'd been lately. Colonel Sanders has been missing you!" Mary and Jody's pet pigeon, Walter, had joined forces with the barn pigeons and only occasionally visited Lucky Foot Stable. As if on cue, Colonel Sanders, the old white rooster, chose just that moment to come strutting into the stable, shaking his floppy red comb. When he spotted Walter perched on Mary's head, he clucked indignantly and

Just as Mary's eyes were about to close, she was jolted awake by a bird landing on her head.

flapped his wings right under Star's nose. Star responded by striking out with his front hoof, almost knocking the Colonel across the aisle.

"Star! Where are your manners?!" Jody exclaimed, slapping him lightly on the shoulder.

"Oh, Colonel, are you OK?" Mary tried to sound sorry, but she couldn't help laughing at the surprised look on the rooster's face as he ruffled his feathers and tried to regain his dignity by perching on the top board of Lady's stall. "Jode, we better get Star out of here. I think he's getting impatient. And Willie said he would meet us on the barn hill by the pickup. He's probably waiting right now, and you know he doesn't like to wait."

Since Mr. Mooney had moved onto the farm, Willie had been free to spend more time training Star, but he still never missed a milking. And now it was only an hour until milking time. Jody unclipped Star from the crossties and fastened the lead rope onto his halter while Mary shook her head to dislodge

Walter, who sailed across the stable to keep
Colonel Sanders company on his perch.

Just as Mary predicted, Willie *was* waiting
at the truck when the girls arrived at the
barn hill, and he didn't look happy about it.

"What in the devil took you two so long?"
he asked grumpily. "If it takes more than an
hour to get that ornery bugger onto the
truck, you're outta luck, because it'll be
milkin' time before you know it."

"Oh, Willie, I don't think it will take that
long," Jody said. "I think Star will be much
easier to load than Lady, because he's just
naturally curious, and I think he'll want to
get on the truck just to see what it's like.
Remember when he got into the truck with
the calves?"

Before Willie could reply, Mary went on,
"And, Willie, I read in a book that inquisi-
tiveness — that means curiosity, I looked it
up — is a sign of intelligence in the colt."

"That's the trouble — he's too smart for his own good," Willie admitted. "Now, quit yer yappin' and get him lined up on the hill there."

Willie had backed the pickup to the barn hill with the tailgate down, so that it made a kind of loading ramp straight into the truck. A thick bed of straw and a mound of green hay with a little grain on top had been placed in the front of the truck bed to tempt Star.

"Now remember how we loaded Lady last time and just do the same thing," Willie instructed.

Jody led Star firmly to the lowered tailgate and walked him straight onto it. When Star's hooves hit the hard surface hidden under the straw, rather than pulling back as Lady had done, he jumped nimbly over the tailgate and landed in the center of the truck bed. Then he lowered his head and began eating the grain as if he had done this every day of his life. Willie quickly raised the tailgate and fastened the homemade rear wood panel first to the tailgate and then to the side panels, and Star's makeshift trailer was secure.

"See, I knew he wouldn't mind," Jody said proudly.

"Still, we need to load him every day until the show, just to be sure," Willie replied wisely. "Now, let him finish that grain and you girls can unload him when he's done. I've got to get to the milk stable and give Roy a hand, and then I'm goin' to town."

Willie and Roy Mooney had become fast friends since the day the dented old pickup truck had arrived at the McMurray farm. And although Willie would never admit it, it was a relief to have some time away from the cows. Annie had also been accepted as a rather mysterious addition to the farm, as Mary and Jody hadn't seen much of her since that first day in the stable. Annie had to spend most of her time watching her little brother, Heath. The two-year-old was a handful, and Annie's older brother Jimmy couldn't help her because he was needed in the barn.

Star finished his grain, and Mary and Jody removed the back panel from the tailgate and propped it gently against the truck. Then they lowered the tailgate and rested it on the barn hill. The instant Star saw from the corner of his eye that there was nothing between him and the hill, he raised his head, turned completely around, jumped out of the truck, and galloped off down the barn hill toward Mr. McMurray's big stone house!

Jody stood with Star's lead rope still in her hand and her mouth open in shock. Mary found her voice first as she flew down the barn hill in pursuit.

"Jody, come on! He's heading toward the road!"

4
Runaway Colt

MARY AND JODY flew as fast as their legs would carry them up the long gravel drive to Mr. McMurray's house. Once in the backyard, they looked in all directions for some sign of Star. But Star was nowhere to be seen.

"I know he ran up this way!" Mary cried. "Oh, I hope he didn't go around the other side of the house and across the road!"

"Mare, don't say that!" Jody said, choking back tears. "Maybe he went over to Willie's house!"

"But we would have seen him run over there. I think we need to check out by the road. Even if he did cross it, he's probably fine. There's not that much traffic."

So the girls galloped to the front yard of the McMurray house and down the bank to the two-lane country road. They stopped at the bottom of the bank where a narrow ditch lay between the yard and the wide shoulder and, shading their eyes from the sun, gazed hopefully at the wheat field across the road — still no sign of the runaway colt.

"I don't think he ran over there, Jode. If he ran into the wheat field, we'd see a path where he knocked the wheat down."

"Well, where could he be then?" Jody asked desperately.

"I don't know. Maybe we should get Mr. McMurray."

So off they ran again to the back of the house. Jody was just about to knock when Mary grabbed her arm and pointed up the lane.

"Jody, look!" she cried.

Jody turned and her mouth flew open in shock for the second time that day. Calmly walking away from the girls and up the lane toward Lucky Foot Stable was Annie Mooney with a dog leash in her hand. And on the end of the dog leash was Star of Wonder, following easily behind and pushing Annie along with his muzzle only once in a while.

"What in the…" Mary began, and then she linked her arm through Jody's and the girls trotted up behind the duo, slowing to a walk as they drew near so as not to spook Star.

"Annie," Jody said quietly as they reached Star's side, "what are you doing?"

"I'm taking Star back to the stable," Annie said matter-of-factly. "He was loose."

"We know he was loose!" Mary yelled. "Didn't you see us looking for him?"

"No, I didn't see you. I was in the trailer and I saw him go flying by the window."

"And then what happened?" Mary asked

Calmly walking away from the girls and up the lane
toward Lucky Foot Stable was Annie Mooney.

patiently. Talking to Annie was sometimes like "pulling hen's teeth," as Willie would say.

"Well, I couldn't do anything right away because I had just put Heath down for a nap. I made sure he was asleep, and then I went outside."

"Then what?" Jody asked after a maddening pause.

"Oh, well, then I saw Star in my backyard eating grass, so I got a carrot."

If Annie stopped talking one more time, Mary was sure she would burst. "Can you tell us the rest of the story, Annie? Did he run away from you?"

"Run away from me? Of course not," Annie snorted. "He came right up and took the carrot and ate it, and then he followed me over to the door of the trailer. I reached inside and got my old dog Buster's dog leash. Buster died a couple years ago, but I kept his leash to remember him by. Sometimes I have to put it on Heath, so he doesn't run away when I take him for walks."

Jody could see from Mary's expression that she really was about to burst, so she took over the questioning.

"So then what happened, Annie? Did Star give you any trouble?"

"Trouble? Of course not," Annie repeated. "He was good as gold."

Mary and Jody could tell that they weren't going to get any more information out of Annie, so they walked in silence the rest of the way back to Lucky Foot Stable. When they reached the open back door, Annie handed the end of the leash to Jody.

"Here you go," she said.

Jody took the leash and turned to walk Star to his stall.

"Thanks a lot, Annie," Mary said generously.

"I need Buster's leash back," Annie replied.

"Oh sure. I'll get it," Mary said, following Jody into the stable. She retrieved the leash and handed it to Annie.

"Well, I guess I'll see you later," Annie

said. She turned and walked back to the house trailer.

Jody joined Mary at the door, and they watched together as Annie opened the squeaky screen door of the trailer and went in.

"I can't figure her out," Jody said.

"I can't figure out how Star got behind the trailer without us seeing him," Jody replied.

"He must have been in Mr. McMurray's front yard when we were in the back, and then when we ran around to the front, he must've gone around the other side of the house and run down to the trailer," Mary surmised.

"I think he ran away in the first place because he's dying for some grass," Jody decided. "I feel bad that Lady and Gypsy get to go out in the pasture with the cows, and Star has to stay in the old dirt paddock and eat hay."

"I know, Jode. But you know Mr. McMurray won't let him out there. He's already mad about Lady and Gypsy 'eating up his prrrofits,'" Mary said, imitating Mr. McMurray's Irish brogue.

"Well, Mr. McMurray lets us walk him around the farm and graze him. He doesn't mind when he eats grass outside of the pasture. Maybe we should tie him out somewhere where he can graze."

Mary nodded, thinking over the possibility. "There's a lot of grass behind the tractor shed," she said. "Let's go back there and see if there's anything to tie him to."

The grass behind the shed grew thick and lush, because it was not fenced in and never used to graze livestock. This is where Mr. McMurray kept all of the farm equipment that wouldn't fit under the roof of the tractor shed. Mary and Jody walked around the open field, eyeing the beautiful grass and looking for a place to tie Star.

"There's really not much open space," Jody observed. "The equipment is too close together."

"I know, but... hey, how about over there?" Mary pointed to a spot at the right corner of the field. There was only one piece of machinery there, and it was surrounded by open spaces of bright green grass.

"That's good, but what can we tie him to?" Jody wondered. "I was hoping there would be a tree or something."

"Well, we can tie him to that thing, whatever it is," Mary replied.

"I think that's what Willie uses to work up the fields," Jody said. "I helped him hook it to the tractor one day. But it's not a plow, it's a… a… I think he called it a springtooth harrow or something like that."

The machinery in question was low to the ground and possessed a series of curved teeth in rows, the blunt points of which rested on the grass.

"See, when Willie gets out to the field he lowers the teeth and they dig up the ground," Jody explained.

"Well, whatever," Mary said impatiently. "I think we could tie Star to this, and he'll have plenty of room to walk all around it and graze to his heart's content. Maybe that's why he's so ornery; he needs some grass to fill up his belly and calm him down."

"It sounds like a good idea, but maybe we should ask Willie first," Jody suggested.

"We can't ask him. He said he was going to town after milking. And besides, he wouldn't mind. Willie always says grass is the best thing for a horse."

So the girls ran back to Lucky Foot Stable and led Star from his stall. They were halfway to the open field when Jody stopped. "Um, Mare, we have everything but the rope! I think we're going to need a rope to tie him out with," she said facetiously.

"Oh yeah," Mary giggled. "Hmmm, let's think."

"I know!" Jody remembered. "There's a long brown rope all curled up and hanging near the hayloft in the barn. I remember seeing it when we were building our hay fort. And it even has a clip on the end!"

"I'll get it!" Mary yelled. Before Jody had even reached the grassy field with Star, Mary was back with the length of rope. The girls led Star through the field of equipment until they came to the place where the harrow sat.

"I know how to tie a slip knot!" Jody bragged. "My dad taught me. Here, Mare, you hold Star and I'll get the rope ready."

Mary allowed Star to drop his head and begin grazing while Jody threaded one end of the rope around a harrow tooth and expertly tied a knot that could easily be untied by pulling on that end, but not the other end, no matter how strongly Star might pull back. Jody clipped the rope to Star's halter, but he was so busy grazing that he didn't even notice the transfer from his lead rope to the long rope.

"See, he was starving for grass," Mary said. "He's going to love this!"

Mary and Jody sat down a short distance away and watched Star wander in a circle, sniffing the grass as if looking for the most succulent blades. Suddenly he turned and blinked at the girls once, raised his head, and looked around. Seeing no fence, and sure that he was free of restraints, he threw up his head and trotted away.

"Uh-oh!" the girls said in unison, jumping up from their seat on the grass. But before they could reach Star, he came to the end of his rope. His head jerked around and he was thrown off balance, but he stayed on his feet. He snorted and shook his head, and the surprised look on his face made the girls laugh in spite of their worry about him breaking his neck.

"Oh, Star, are you OK?" Jody said sympathetically, patting him on the shoulder.

"Good thing he didn't get up much speed," Mary observed. "I think he knows now that he's tied. But we'd better watch him for a while to be sure."

So the girls sat down once again and watched Star go back to grazing. He didn't try another trot, but occasionally he would come to the end of the rope at a walk. When he realized he could go no further, he would turn quietly and go another route.

"He's getting the hang of it now," Jody said proudly. "He is so smart!"

"I think we could leave him out overnight, don't you?" Mary suggested. "I've got to get home soon, and so do you. It would be a shame to take him in so soon, when he's enjoying himself so much. And he understands the rope now, I think."

"Hmmm, I don't know, Mare. Do you think he'll be OK?" Jody worried.

"Sure he will. We'll be back first thing in the morning. He can eat all this grass down tonight, and tomorrow we'll tie him someplace else. I really think the grass will help him calm down, and then he'll be good for the show next week!"

"Well, OK," Jody agreed, "but we've got to get him a bucket of water. Help me carry it over from the stable."

So the girls carried the water, one on each side of the bucket, to Star's grazing spot. They watched him a little longer to make sure he was concentrating on grazing and not escaping, and then rode home on their bikes in the summer twilight.

5

Trouble in the Field

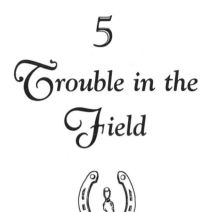

☝HE NEXT MORNING dawned bright and sunny, and Mary and Jody, by pre-arrangement, met earlier than usual at Lucky Foot Stable. The instant their bikes were parked on the gravel lane, they were off to the grassy field behind Mr. McMurray's tractor shed to check on Star.

"I wonder if he drank all his water," Mary said as the girls skipped across the lane toward the shed. "We'll have to get the bucket and fill it up again."

"I think we should bring him in right away and try loading him again, like Willie said," Jody suggested. "He left the truck parked on the barn hill for us."

The first thing the girls noticed when they rounded the corner of the shed was that the water bucket had been knocked over. The second thing they noticed was that Star was lying down.

"Star!" Mary called across the field. "Get up, you lazybones!"

"That's funny, Mare… he usually doesn't lie down like…" Jody stopped in mid-sentence. Something about the way Star was lying there didn't look right, and both girls knew it at the same instant. Without another word, they took off at a dead run across the field.

The reason for Star's unnatural position was horribly revealed as the girls approached. The long rope they had used to tie him to the springtooth harrow was now wrapped over and around and through the teeth of the machine until it had gotten so short that Star was thrown to the ground and trapped, not able to stand or move. Under his feet, the grass had been reduced to bare dirt where he had fought to get up. His cheek was resting on the flat side of one of the teeth, and he was groaning low in his throat.

"Star!" Mary and Jody screamed, dropping to their knees.

"Oh no, oh no, oh no, oh no," Jody wailed, tugging in vain on the slipknot, which had tightened beyond her strength during the struggle. "Mary, go get Willie!"

Mary was gone in a flash. Jody gave up on the slipknot and tried to unhook the snap from Star's halter, but it was twisted and un-yielding. As she worked, Star looked up at her desperately and tried again to get his legs under him.

"Shhh, boy, don't move, don't move," Jody sobbed, stroking the side of his head. "Willie will be here soon."

No sooner had the words passed Jody's

No sooner had the words passed Jody's lips than the rope binding Star to the harrow was cut.

lips than the rope binding Star to the harrow was cut just below his halter ring with one swift motion. Willie jammed the blade of his pocketknife into the ground and gently lifted Star's head so that his cheek was away from the harrow tooth. Mary and Jody gripped each other's hands, watching Willie with tears streaming down their cheeks as he cradled the colt's head in his arms and stroked his neck.

"Come on, buddy, you'll be alright," Willie murmured, running his hand down Star's front legs, feeling along the cannon bone and pasterns. Star rested his head on Willie's leg and moaned once more, exhausted from his nightlong struggle with the harrow.

"You girls, go get a smaller bucket from the milk stable," Willie instructed, "and put a little water in it. He needs a drink. Then we'll try to get him up."

The girls were back with the water in an instant. Willie supported Star's head while Jody held the bucket to his lips and Mary looked on, saying a silent prayer. Star raised his head a little higher, sniffing listlessly at the water.

"C'mon, boy, just take a little sip," Mary whispered. "You've got to."

Star lipped at the water once more, then he lowered his muzzle and took a real drink.

"Good boy, good boy," Jody murmured through her tears. Willie rubbed Star's neck and shoulder vigorously in an effort to get the circulation going and encourage him to stand.

"That's enough water, Jody," he said gruffly. "That should perk him up. Now stand back so he has room to get his legs under him."

Jody obeyed Willie's order just in time to avoid being hit by Star's front hooves.

He suddenly sat up on his haunches and stretched them in front of him, searching for the strength to push himself up from the slippery grass. He groaned once more from the effort, his muzzle lowered almost to the ground.

"Here, Jody, you stand at his head and hold onto his halter," Willie instructed. "I'm gonna give him a little help from behind. Just watch out for his front feet when he goes to stand up."

Willie crouched behind Star, and while Jody tugged gently on his halter, Willie lifted the struggling colt's haunches with all his strength. Star rocked to and fro once more, and then with a grunt from deep in his chest, he hoisted himself to his feet.

Mary and Jody refrained themselves from throwing their arms around his neck, afraid their weight would knock him over in his weakened state. He stood with his head down, snorting low through his nostrils while they stroked him softly on the shoulder. Willie was busy going from one leg to the next, running his fingers along the fine bones and searching for injuries.

"Oh, Star, I'm so sorry," Jody whispered. "I didn't know you would get all tangled up like that!"

"Willie, is he alright?" Mary asked fearfully. "Did he break anything?"

"Don't look like it, but it's a wonder," Willie said. "Lucky he didn't get himself thrown down on top of the thing. Then you woulda had a mess. Now would one of you mind tellin' me what the idea was of tyin' him out here all night long with nobody watchin' him?"

Mary and Jody looked at their feet. Before they could answer, Willie continued, "First, you never tie any horse, a young'un especially, to a piece of machinery. In fact, you never tie them out to anything unless you're there to watch them. Second, you never put a horse out on grass for that much time unless you get his stomach used to it first. You're lucky he didn't founder. Must've got tangled up early in the night, 'cause if he had grazed all night long, you'd have a ruined colt right now."

No reply from Mary or Jody.

"Now it looks like he's gonna be alright — no broken bones or even any cuts or bruises.

He's just worn out from tryin' to get himself on his feet all night. See if he'll walk with you, Jody, and we'll get him back to the stable."

Jody took a step and tugged gently on the lead rope. At first, Star simply stretched out his muzzle and sniffed her, unwilling to move.

"Don't stand so close, and give him a little more rope. Let him want to follow you, rather than pullin' on him," Willie suggested.

Jody walked forward until she was holding the very end of the lead rope and stood patiently, waiting until Star felt ready to walk with her. He lowered his head and sniffed the ground.

"Come on, boy," Jody encouraged quietly, giving the gentlest of tugs on the rope. Star shook his head and finally took a tentative step forward, then another, until he was walking stiffly and laboriously behind Jody. Mary and Willie walked along beside them until the four of them reached Lucky Foot Stable and Star was safely inside his stall.

"Now we've got to keep an eye on him all day and look for any swellin' in his legs," Willie said, watching as Star drank a little more water from his bucket. "In fact it might be a good idea to hose his legs down with some cold water to keep the swellin' from startin' to begin with. Mary, I want you to make up a hot bran mash, about half a scoop with a little molasses in it, and let him have that. And Jody, get a soft brush and brush him real gentle to see if you can find any sore spots, that way you can tell if there might be some bruises we can't see. Then we can rub him with a little liniment to help his sore muscles."

Before Willie could finish his sentence, Mary was at the feed bin scooping up bran and Jody was selecting the softest brush she could find from her tack trunk. She went to Star and ran the brush tenderly over his whole body, mindful of any flinching he might do if she hit a sore spot. Miraculously, Star seemed fine except for a tender spot on the side of his head where it had rested on the harrow tooth and another on his shoulder where he must have rubbed it on the ground while struggling to stand. He even rubbed his head up and down, up and down on Jody's arm just like he always did.

"Oh, Star, don't be nice to me. I don't deserve it," Jody cried, trying again to choke back her tears. "I promise I will never leave you alone again!"

"You can leave him alone, just not tied out," Willie said matter-of-factly. "Now there's no use cryin' over spilt milk. Lucky for everybody, he's not really hurt. He'll be feeling fine in a few days if you girls take good care of him."

"Willie!" Mary exclaimed suddenly. "What about the horse show? Can Star still go?"

"We'll just have to see how he feels. I don't see why not, if he gets over his soreness by then. Maybe somethin' good'll come out of this, you never know."

"Something good from this?" Jody asked

incredulously. "What do you mean, Willie? How could anything good come out of this?"

"Well, I've seen it happen before, where somethin' traumatic happens to a youngster, or even to an older horse, and it seems to calm them down," Willie said, tugging on his ear lobe. "I don't want to say his spirit is broken, but it might just be a little more relaxed. He might be ready to get over his ornery streak and get on about his business. We'll just have to see."

Mary and Jody silently took in this bit of information and stood watching as Star sniffed at the hot bran mash, and then, discovering a nice lump of molasses, began to eat with almost as much enthusiasm as he ever did.

"See there, he's feelin' better already. You'd have to worry about him if he didn't want to eat," Willie said wisely. "Now, when he's done, we'll take him out and hose down his legs for a few minutes then rub his muscles with some liniment. We'll keep him in his stall tonight, but we'll turn him out in the paddock tomorrow so he can walk around. That'll keep him from gettin' stiff."

"Thanks ever so, Willie. I don't know what we would have done if you hadn't been here," Mary said gratefully.

"Well, did you learn anything?"

"Oh yes," Jody said. "I learned a lot. But mostly I learned not to do anything we're not sure of until we ask you first."

"Good idea," Willie said, and he smiled for the first time that morning. "Now get your rubbin' rag out, and fetch me that liniment."

6
Making Star Beautiful

By the time Friday came, Star was almost back to his old self. His muscles were no longer sore thanks to a daily liniment rub, and his cheek and shoulder were not as tender to Jody's touch. The only change the girls could detect was in the colt's personality. Just as Willie had predicted, Star was no longer apt to get in an ornery mood. He did everything Mary and Jody asked of him, even trotting nicely around the ring. And when it was time for his lesson on squaring up, he was willing to try, although this was something he had trouble understanding.

"OK, Jody, let's try it again," Mary instructed from the sidelines of the ring (which was really just the paddock). Finnegan sat at Mary's feet, and Jody, a thin longe whip in her hand, held Star at the end of his lead rope. "Hold his head up a little higher and tap his right front fetlock with the longe whip — it's not quite in place yet."

The idea was to get all four legs in a square position — the two front legs side by side and squarely under the body, and the two hind legs the same with the head slightly elevated, ears up, looking attentive and content. The problem was, whenever Star would get the hind two legs square, the front two would be out of line. And when the front two were perfect, the hind two were slightly askew. And when his head was just right, all four legs were off! Jody took Mary's suggestion and tapped Star lightly on the fetlock with the end of the longe whip. Star obediently moved the leg into position. All four legs were in line! But then he lifted his right hind foot to kick at a fly on his belly, and when the foot came down, it was all wrong!

"I give up, Mare," Jody said, throwing the whip down in frustration. "He's really trying, but he just can't get it! It's getting late, and the show is tomorrow! What are we going to do?"

"Well, we're going to take him to the show, of course. I'm sure he won't be the only yearling colt that doesn't know how to square up. He's really good at everything else, like trotting around the ring and standing quietly, even if his legs aren't perfect. You'll see, he'll do fine. Remember when you were so worried about riding Lady in a show? And you won first place!"

"I know, I know. I guess I should just quit worrying about winning and make it a learning experience," Jody decided. "It'll be fun, right?"

Finnegan sat at Mary's feet, and Jody, a longe whip in her hand, held Star at the end of his lead rope.

"Yes. But winning wouldn't hurt either! Now let's take Star in and give him one last inspection. If he doesn't behave tomorrow, at least he'll look good while he's being bad," Mary giggled. "Come on, Finney, you can help us."

So Star was given a pat on the neck for effort and led into the aisle of the stable where Jody put him on crossties. Finnegan lay down on the cool dirt floor while Mary and Jody stood back and gazed at Star with a critical eye.

"Get the scissors, Jode, I think I see a few long hairs that need to be trimmed," Mary commanded. Willie had instructed the girls about grooming the colt for the show ring, and they had been practicing for weeks, trimming Star's whiskers and fetlocks and bridle path of long hair. They had even clipped a little of the hair from inside his ears with electric clippers to get him used to the noise and had given him several baths under Willie's supervision. Now Mary trimmed a few stray hairs from Star's muzzle while Jody put the finishing touches on his already shiny coat with a soft brush.

"Now we should pack the tack box with all the stuff we'll need tomorrow," Jody suggested, when they were satisfied that Star looked his best.

"Now just hold yer horses," Willie's voice came from the doorway of the stable. "There's one more thing we need to do before tomorrow. Should've done it before this, but I never had the time to show you till now. You can't have this old straggly mane in the show ring."

"Straggly mane! But Willie, I've been training it so it's all on one side, and I just combed it!" Jody replied indignantly.

"Yes, and it looks right good, but it's a little too long. It needs to be pulled."

"Pulled? What do you mean?" asked Jody.

"I know, Jode," Mary grinned. "I read it in a book. You take a pulling comb and twist the long hairs of the mane around it, and then you yank them out."

Jody's mouth flew open in shock, as Willie shook his head and shot Mary a stern look.

"Mary, hush. You work on real small sections at a time, and you do pull them out, but the horse doesn't feel any pain. They have hardly any nerves in the crest of the neck where the hair grows. He shouldn't mind it a bit once he gets used to the feel of it."

"But, Willie, his mane is so pretty. It's black and white hairs all mixed together. I've never seen another one like it, even in books!" Jody protested.

"Now, it'll still look just as good, just a little shorter, that's all. The judge will like it better that way. We have to even it up so it's all the same length, and it'll be easier to bathe, too. Don't forget you have to get up early and give him a bath in the morning."

The girls groaned in unison at this reminder, but Jody dutifully went to her tack box, took out the metal wide-toothed comb she used to comb Star's unruly mane, and handed it to Willie.

"Well, go ahead," she said glumly.

"That's not the right comb, Jody," Mary said smugly. "I told you, you have to have a *pulling* comb."

"But I don't have a *pulling* comb!" Jody said in frustration. "I don't even know what a pulling comb looks like!"

"Looks like this," Willie said, taking a small metal comb with very short teeth placed close together from his overalls pocket and holding it up for the girls to see. Star extended his muzzle and sniffed curiously at the funny-looking tool. "Now, you just start with a little section of mane and tease some of it up with the comb," Willie murmured, demonstrating the technique as he spoke. "Then wrap the long hairs you want to get rid of around the comb and pull them out," he continued. And with that, Willie jerked quickly on the comb and the long mane hairs pulled out easily still wrapped around the little teeth. Star startled slightly at the feeling of pressure and the quick movement of the comb, but his ears stayed up. He turned and looked at Willie as if to say, "Hey — this is something new!"

"Willie!" Jody grimaced, putting her hand to her mouth. "Are you sure that doesn't hurt?"

"Does it look like it hurts?" Willie asked, patting Star on the neck. "It felt a little funny to him the first time, but watch, he's getting used to it already," he continued, expertly wrapping the next section of mane around the comb and pulling out more strands of hair. The girls watched in silence as Willie worked his way along Star's mane with the comb until it all lay evenly on his neck, shorter by a few inches. When at last he came to the base of Star's neck, Willie re-placed the comb in his pocket and stood back to examine his handiwork.

"Look, Jode — Star's asleep!" Mary

whispered. The girls giggled as Star's head dropped lower and lower until the crossties seemed to be holding him up and his nose almost touched the dirt floor of Lucky Foot Stable.

"See, it hurt him so much he dropped right off," Willie said sarcastically.

"Thanks, Willie. It does look better, I guess," Jody acknowledged. "Oh, I just know Star is going to be the prettiest colt at the whole show!"

"Pretty or not, he just better behave himself," Willie growled. "Now you better get all your stuff gathered up for tomorrow. I don't want to be waitin' on you in the mornin'."

Willie gently patted Star awake and led him into his stall, while the girls bustled around Lucky Foot Stable gathering up the rest of their show supplies. Since they wouldn't be riding Star, they didn't need a saddle or bridle. But they did need a soft brush, a hard brush, a mane and tail comb, a rubber curry, and a hoofpick. These were all scrubbed clean and packed neatly in the little tack box. Saddle soap was added to buff up his leather halter if necessary, and hoof dressing thrown in to make his hooves shine. Jody carefully found a spot for the horse shampoo and scrubby mitt for bathing. Last to be tucked safely into the box was the soft leather lead shank with a brass plate reading, "Star of Wonder." Jody's father had given this to Jody as a gift when Star was born. When the tack box was full, the girls stood back and gazed at it with a contented sigh. "Now, where am I going to put these towels?" Mary asked herself, holding up two fluffy blue towels, one in each hand, for drying Star after his bath.

"Um, Mare… there's one problem," Jody said sheepishly.

"What? Are you still worrying about Star squaring up?"

"Nooo… I'm just wondering why we packed the bathing stuff in the tack box and why you're worrying about where to put the towels when we're giving Star a bath *before* we go to the show," she said with a grin.

Mary didn't reply, but looked first at one towel and then the other. "Hmmph," she giggled. "I guess we didn't think of that."

The girls looked at each other and giggled again. The week had been very long and nerve-wracking, and the training had been frustrating. Mary and Jody were tired. Their giggles turned into full-blown laughter and they were off on a laughing jag until tears ran down their cheeks. Finnegan joined in by barking and turning in circles, and Willie just shook his head and hobbled out the stable door.

"I think we'd better go home and go to bed," Mary suggested through her tears. "We're so tired we can't think straight."

"And we have to get up early," Jody added, wiping her cheeks. "Willie said to be here by five, so Star would have time to dry before we go. Are you sure your mom said it's OK for me to stay at your house?"

"Of course it's OK. And she even said

she would drive us up here in the morning, so we wouldn't have to ride our bikes so early. I think she feels guilty, because she has to work and can't come to the show."

"I know, my dad can't go either. He promised he'd come to the next one."

So the girls filled Star's water bucket, gave him another flake of hay, and said good-bye. They were both ready for a good night's sleep. The day they had been waiting for was almost here at last.

7
Final Touches

IT WAS STILL dark when Mary's mother dropped the girls off at Lucky Foot Stable the next morning. She gave them a hug for good luck and three paper sacks (one each for Mary and Jody, and one for Willie) filled with goodies for lunch. When they entered the stable and turned on the light, Star raised his head and blinked sleepily, swiveling his ears and cocking his head as if to say, "What in the world are you doing here so early?" From his perch on the top board of Lady's stall, Colonel Sanders shook his head and flapped his wings indignantly. Then, in protest of the early hour, he stretched out his neck, opened his beak to the ceiling, and crowed over and over again.

"Alright, alright, Colonel, we hear you. We're awake already," Mary said, covering her ears. "Star, how would you like a treat to start off your big day?"

Mary took a shiny red apple from her lunch bag and twisted it in her hands until it split in half. She held one half between her front teeth and offered the other half to Star on the flat of her palm. Star sniffed the treat for only an instant before taking the whole thing in his mouth and chewing hungrily, apple juice dripping from his lips.

"Mare, I don't think your mom packed that apple for Star to eat," Jody giggled.

"It's OK," Mary slurped. She took the apple half from between her clenched teeth and held it out to Jody. "I only wanted half anyway. Want a bite?" she offered.

"No, thanks, I have my own," Jody replied. "We'd better get Star out and get him ready for his bath. Willie will be here before you know it."

"I know. I'm so glad he doesn't have to milk this morning and can come to the show with us!"

"We ain't gonna git to the show if you two don't quit gabbin' and get that colt washed," Willie said, appearing suddenly in the open doorway.

"Willie! You're early, aren't you?" Jody said, leading Star from his stall. Before Willie could reply, Mary groaned at the sight of the right side of Star's body, only then fully visible in the fluorescent light of the aisle.

"Oh no!" she exclaimed. "Star, what have you done?"

Willie hobbled around to the side in question while Jody turned Star's head to the left so she could get a good look. Then it was her turn to moan in dismay. Almost the entire right side of Star's body from front leg to back was covered with a greenish-brown stain that could only have been acquired by the tired colt lying down in his stall overnight in a fresh pile of manure.

"Willie! What are we going to do?" wailed Jody. "We'll never get that cleaned off in time for the show!"

"If you quit your whinin' and gather up some rags we will. Mary, git a lead rope and git him over to the milk house where we can hook up some warm water," Willie ordered. "Why do you think I had you two git up here so early? Just in case somethin' like this happened."

Jody grabbed the horse shampoo, two scrubby mitts, and a handful of rags the girls had cut from old towels and followed Mary and Star up the gravel driveway. By the time they reached the milk house, Willie was standing outside the door with a hose and spray nozzle hooked up to the warm water spigot and was testing the water temperature on his open palm.

Star cocked his head and peered warily at the gentle spray, sidestepping and almost landing on Mary's foot.

"Star, please behave. You've had baths before," Mary pleaded.

"Just hold him still and let me get him used to the spray first," Willie instructed. Mary turned Star in a circle and led him as close to the hose as she could. Willie sprayed water on the grass in a circle in front of Star and then slowly moved the spray closer and closer until it played around Star's hooves. Star snorted and stomped at the water but didn't try to move from Mary's grasp. The sun was just beginning to cast its light on the day as Willie moved the warm spray gently up Star's front legs. When the water reached his chest, he lowered his head and opened his mouth to the spray, then lifted his muzzle to the sky and raised his lip as horses do when they smell something funny.

"Well, I guess he's not scared of it," Willie chuckled. "Jody, git a bucket from the milk house and fill it up with warm water, and git your shampoo and scrubbers ready. I'll finish wettin' him down in the meantime."

Jody was back in an instant with the bucket of warm water, carefully setting it down on the dewy grass. She picked up one of the scrubby mitts and put it on over her hand.

"OK, Jody, get some of that shampoo on the mitt and just start scrubbin' in a circle, first on his shoulder, and keep rinsin' out your mitt, especially when you hit the green spots," Willie instructed.

"Oh, Willie can I scrub, too?" pleaded Mary. Willie silently took the lead rope from Mary's hand and watched as the girls scrubbed in circles, rinsing their mitts in the bucket and replenishing the shampoo each time. Soon Star was a big greenish soapy mess, but he seemed to be enjoying himself, stretching out his front legs and nipping playfully at the girls as they scrubbed.

"OK, Willie, time to rinse him off," Mary announced, standing back to admire their soaping job. But before she could take the rope from Willie's hand, Star planted his feet, snorted once, and shook himself heartily, showering the girls and Willie from head to toe with greenish soapsuds.

"Daggone ornery bugger!" Willie shouted, wiping the soap from his face. Mary and Jody dissolved in a fit of giggles when Willie picked up the hose and began to squirt Star with it, not nearly so gently this time.

"Willie! He didn't mean it!" Mary laughed, shaking her hands to get the soap off.

"Quit yer gigglin' and go get a sweat scraper so we can get this extra water off. Get a tail comb too. And Jody, git yer rags ready to give him a good rubdown. Looks like most of the manure stains came off," Willie said, continuing the spray over Star's back and down his hind legs until the foam completely disappeared. Star arched his back at the feel of the water and stretched out his front legs like a dog enjoying a good scratching, clearly enjoying his bath.

Star shook himself heartily, showering the girls and Willie from head to toe with greenish soapsuds.

Mary returned with the metal sweat scraper and Jody stepped up with a terry cloth rag in each hand. Without a word Mary applied the blunt-edged scraper to Star's neck and moved downward to his shoulder and then along his barrel and belly, "scraping" the excess water from his coat as she went. Jody followed close behind with the rags, rubbing vigorously in a circular motion until her rags were sopping wet and she had to go for more. Willie watched in silence, Star's lead rope in hand, and Star stretched out his neck as though this was his day at the spa. When Mary reached Star's tail, she put down the sweat scraper and picked up the plastic tail comb, running it through the wet tangles until they were all smoothed out. Jody wrung out her last rag and gently wiped Star's nostrils and the corners of his eyes.

"Well, he looks a lot better than he did a half hour ago," Willie observed dryly. "Walk him back over to the stable and keep him walkin' in the sun until he dries some more.

I'll put the hose away and get the truck ready."

Jody took the lead rope from Willie's grasp, while Mary hung the wet rags over the fence to dry.

"Mare, don't forget to gather up all the bathing supplies," Jody called over her shoulder as she turned Star toward Lucky Foot Stable.

"Since when did I get to be the groom?" Mary muttered good-naturedly, gathering up the supplies as fast as she could and taking off at a trot to catch up to Jody and Star.

"I didn't realize how sunny it is already," Mary panted when she reached Star's side. "Are we going to be late?"

The girls had been so busy working on Star that they hadn't noticed how far the sun had risen and how quickly the morning was getting away from them.

"Willie, are we going to be late?" Jody called to Willie who was on the barn hill getting the truck ready for Star. "Is Star's class in the very beginning of the day?"

"Close to, but we still have time. We won't be as early as I wanted to be, but we'll make it," Willie called back, hobbling down the hill and casting a critical eye on Star's gleaming coat. "I reckon he looks alright. But there's one thing you forgot."

Willie didn't say any more; he just turned and walked back up the barn hill toward the truck. Mary and Jody looked at Star, then they looked at each other, then looked back at Star again, trying to remember what they had forgotten. Finally Jody's eyes traveled to Star's hooves.

"The hoof dressing!" Jody exclaimed. "Mare, can you get it out of the tack trunk? Oh, and we forgot to wrap his tail! The wrap is in the trunk too!"

Star stood perfectly still while the dressing was applied, and he only moved around a little while Mary wrapped his tail in a stretchy bandage to keep it clean. Then it was time to load.

Mary led Star to the barn hill where Willie had carefully backed the truck. Willie lowered the tailgate so that it was resting flat on the side of the hill, making a ramp for Star. The girls had practiced loading and unloading him — making sure he didn't run away again — several times in the past week when he felt up to it. Now the open tailgate was a familiar sight, and Star walked easily into the pickup bed and dropped his head to eat the hay and grain placed there. Jody ran back into the stable to gather up her show clothes while Mary made one last inspection of the tack box to make sure they weren't forgetting anything, and they were finally off to the show!

8
At the Show

"YOU'RE NOT NERVOUS, are you, Jody?" asked Mary as they jounced over the bumpy back road that led to the horse show. Jody had been silent for most of the ride, and as they neared the showgrounds, Mary thought it was time to break the ice.

"I am, but not nearly as nervous as I was when we took Lady to the show," Jody replied quietly. "At least this time I don't have to ride. And I know what to expect now. And besides, it's just for the fun and experience.

It's Star's first show, and if he doesn't win anything, there's always next time."

Mary nodded and Willie smiled at Jody's good judgment. As they rounded a bend in the road, a field full of horse trailers became visible, and Willie slowed to a stop at the hand-lettered sign reading, "HORSE SHOW." Careful not to jostle Star, Willie put on his signal and turned slowly onto the long farm lane, and then he crept along, looking for a low hill to back up to for the unloading. As it turned out, Willie had to drive all the way to the end of the lane, where a bank barn much like the one on the McMurray farm sat at the top of an inviting knoll.

"Mary, why don't you get out and guide me back, and Jody, get ready to put the tailgate down," Willie said, looking at his pocket watch. "We don't have a lotta time."

Even before Willie had finished his sentence, the girls were out of the truck, Mary waving Willie back to the perfect spot on the hill and Jody poised to bring the tailgate down as soon as the truck was in position. In a flash, Star was led from the makeshift trailer and down the hill.

"Now, just walk him around to get the kinks out of his legs while I find a place to park," Willie instructed. "Then you'd better git entered in your classes."

Star lifted his head and gazed curiously in all directions — ears up and sniffing the air. He had only been off the farm once before, and that excursion had been a terrible mistake.

"I hope Star doesn't have any bad memories of his last trip away from the barn," Mary commented. "Maybe we should take him down to the ring, so he can see it and get used to the idea. We still have a little time before we have to enter our classes."

"Good idea," Jody agreed, turning toward the outdoor ring where a class was in progress. As the girls neared the ring, they saw a group of about ten young horses lined up for inspection. The judge paced up and down the front of the line, jotting down notes on a clipboard and occasionally stopping to speak to one of the competitors.

"Look, Jody — these are just babies! This must be the weanling class. They sure aren't squared up!"

"Or even standing still," Jody observed. It was all the handlers could do to get the weanlings to stop fidgeting and pawing when the judge approached.

"Star, you can do better than that!" Mary assured the colt. But Star wasn't listening to Mary. As he caught sight of the ring full of babies, he flung up his head, snorted once, and let out a joyful whinny of greeting.

"Star, shhhhhh!" Jody warned. But it was too late. At the sound of Star's hello, the weanlings became agitated, some whinnying back, some turning in circles, but all devoting their full attention to the black-and-white colt by the side of the ring. The competitors and even the judge turned to determine the cause of the disturbance.

"Uh-oh," Jody began, but she was cut short by a gnarly hand pulling the lead rope from her grasp. She looked up to see Willie turning Star abruptly from the ring.

"Didn't I tell ya to get over there and enter your classes?" he hissed, hobbling away from the ring as fast as he could go with Star in tow and the embarrassed girls trailing behind. "You don't bring a horse down by a ring when a class is goin' on, especially a ring full of weanlings. Haven't I taught you anything?"

"Sorry, Willie," Jody squeaked. "We thought it would be good to get him used to it."

"Oh, ya did, huh? Well, if you don't get over there and sign up, you'll miss your classes altogether, and there won't be any reason to get him used to anything. And Jody, are you plannin' on changin' your clothes anytime soon?"

Without another word, Mary headed to the entry booth and filled out the paperwork for two yearling classes, while Jody retrieved her show clothes from the truck and changed into them in the bathroom of the barn.

"I got your number, Jode. Your first class is grooming and showmanship," Mary informed Jody as she emerged from the bathroom. "Wow! You look good," she continued, surveying Jody's outfit of white blouse, tan pants, green tie, and black paddock boots.

"I don't know how I'm going to stay clean," Jody wondered while Mary tied the cardboard number around Jody's waist. "I wanted to give Star one last going-over before the class. Willie said the judge is really picky about any dust or dirt they find on the coat. And they ask if you groomed the colt yourself, so it has to be me."

"I think you could do that and stay clean," Mary observed. "We scrubbed him so well at the farm that he shouldn't have a speck of dirt on him! I'll get the mane and tail comb and the soft brush."

Mary was right — even with the vigorous

last-minute brushing Jody gave Star's coat, hardly a speck of dust could be raised. And his mane and tail only needed a quick combing. Willie walked in a circle around the handsome colt, looking him over with a practiced eye, finally nodding his approval with one reservation.

"You're forgettin' one thing, ain't you?" he asked cryptically, eyeing Star's leather lead shank as a hint.

"The saddle soap! We almost forgot!" Mary cried, retrieving the can of leather cleaner from the little tack box. "Jody, I'll do his lead shank, and you use the saddle soap to wipe your boots one last time, and then we'll be ready!"

A moment later the announcer's voice came clearly over the sound system. "The next class is class number three, yearling grooming and showmanship. Please be ready with your yearlings at ring number one."

"Oh no! Wait, wait, I'm almost done," Mary cried, rushing to buff up the brown leather shank with a soft cloth. There wasn't time to do Jody's boots, but they had been shined back at the barn and still looked fine. Willie stood by and observed, having decided that the girls should get Star ready for his class on their own. Finally he interrupted their frantic last-minute preparations.

"Alright, he looks as good as he's ever gonna. You better git over to the ring before you miss the class altogether," he directed.

"OK, Willie. Now, Jody, don't forget to smile at the judge, answer all his questions, hold Star's head up, try to square him up the best you can, oh, and don't be nervous," Mary babbled breathlessly, striding along beside Jody and Star on the way to the ring.

"Mary, I'm not nervous. Not like last time. Star will be fine," Jody said, glancing proudly at the colt prancing beside her.

And Star *was* fine. Mary and Willie watched at ringside as Jody led him easily through the gate and to the fence rail as if he had been showing all his life. The judge, a tall gray-haired man with a clipboard in his hand, first asked the handlers to walk their yearlings around the ring, staying close to the rail, while he wrote down each of the numbers of the nine entrants. Willie squinted at the number displayed on Jody's back as she led Star past.

"I see Jody's number is thirty-four," he said to Mary. "Ain't that the same number she had when she showed Lady?"

Mary looked at the number, then at Willie, and screwed up her face in thought. "I think it is, Willie!" she finally exclaimed. "It *was* number thirty-four! It's a good omen!"

"Might be a bad omen, considerin' what happened at that show," Willie mumbled, but Mary had turned her full attention to the goings-on in the ring. The judge had instructed the handlers to line the yearlings up across the ring in a row facing him. Star happened to end up third in line, but even with colts and fillies close on either side of him, he stood quietly, only occasionally gazing curiously to his left and right. The judge gestured for the first yearling in line, a lively bay colt, to come forward. He instructed the handler to trot the colt along the fence line to the end of the ring and then turn and trot back again. The bay colt picked up a nice high-stepping trot going down the ring, but when the handler turned him, he sidestepped, snorted, and flung up his head, yanking the lead shank completely from the handler's grasp!

"Uh-oh, Willie, there he goes!" Mary exclaimed as the bay colt took off at a jouncy trot around the ring — tail up, nostrils flaring, whinnying at the other yearlings as if to say, "Hey, I'm free! Why don't you join me?"

The other yearlings responded by pulling on their own lead shanks and pawing the ground, some whinnying back as they watched the judge and the handler attempt to corner the frisky colt. Star was no exception. Jody did her best to hold him as he turned in a circle and whinnied gleefully to the runaway colt. Finally the judge and handler, their arms outstretched, managed to herd the outlaw into a corner of the ring, where he decided to stand quietly and let himself be caught.

"That's always the way with weanling and yearling classes," said a voice by the rail. "One or two of 'em will misbehave and rile everybody else up. Too bad it was the first one in line."

Mary and Willie turned to find the source of the comment — a man in jeans and cowboy hat, leaning over the rail and chewing on a piece of straw. Mary thought the man looked vaguely familiar, but she couldn't place him. Willie's reply brought her memory back vividly.

"Hey there, good to see you again," Willie said, shaking the man's hand. "We've got a colt in this class today because of you." As Willie pointed Star out to the man, Mary suddenly remembered where she had seen him before. He was the driver of the truck that had taken Star to the slaughterhouse by accident the year before.

The bay colt took off at a jouncy trot around the ring, tail up, nostrils flaring, and whinnying.

"Well, I'll be… I remember that colt now. He got himself in quite a jam that day."

"And you told us about this show. Nice place you got here," Willie commented. "This here is one of the girls that was goin' crazy that day looking for the ornery bugger," he continued. "And the other one is handlin' the colt."

Their attention was once more drawn to the ring, where the second entry, a palomino filly, had just finished her trot for the judge. The runaway bay colt was back in line and behaving himself, but he had caused a lasting disturbance to the other yearlings in the ring, all of whom were now a little more nervous and fidgety because of his antics. Star had settled down somewhat and was standing fairly quietly, but Jody's attempts to square him up were in vain.

"Oh well," Mary sighed, "he doesn't look any worse than some of the others."

Just as Mary finished her comment, the

judge pointed at Jody to bring Star out and trot him down the fence line. Seeing the nervousness on Jody's face, Mary tried to send her friend a telepathic message.

"Don't worry about the commotion, Jode. You weren't nervous before; you shouldn't be nervous now," she whispered as Jody and Star began their trot. Mary breathed a sigh of relief as Star trotted nicely down to the end of the ring and back again, his head held high. She noticed that the smile had returned to Jody's face as the judge motioned for them to step back in line.

"That is a right nice looking colt," the owner of the farm commented to Willie. "If he doesn't get placed in this class, he sure should in the conformation class. Well, good luck now."

Willie and Mary were left alone at ringside to watch the rest of the class in silence. There were no more problems as each yearling performed at the trot. Then it was time for the judge to go down the line, questioning each exhibitor and examining each yearling for good grooming.

Jody faced Star as she waited for the judge and pulled gently on his halter in another attempt to square him up, this time more successfully. His hind legs were slightly askew, but he was almost perfect in front.

"Please stay that way; please stay that way," she prayed silently as the judge approached her, looking down at his clipboard.

"Number thirty-four?"

"Yes, sir," Jody replied, lifting Star's head slightly to give the judge a better look at him.

"What is your name and the name of your colt?"

"Jody Stafford, sir, and this is Star of Wonder," she said proudly.

"And his date of birth?" he asked.

"He was born on Christmas Eve, sir. He's a year-and-a-half old."

"Hmmph — Christmas Eve? Funny time for a foal to be born. Usually happens in the spring."

"Yes, sir. Well, it was quite a surprise," Jody answered, smiling.

"Do you know the name of his dam?"

"His dam's name is Lady, sir," Jody replied.

"Lady…?"

"Just Lady, sir."

"And his sire?"

"Uh," Jody stammered. "Um, I'm not sure of the name of his sire."

The judge was silent then as he ran his hand down the crest of Star's mane to see if he could raise any dust. He walked in a circle around Star just as Willie had done, surveying him with a critical eye. He nodded once and patted him on the rump. Then he turned to Jody.

"Could you pick up his right front foot for me?" The judge asked.

Jody leaned down and ran her hand down Star's right front leg. He immediately picked up his foot and stood quietly while Jody held it.

"Thank you. That's all," the judge said.

He jotted some notes on his clipboard and went on to the next yearling.

Mary caught Jody's eye from the sidelines and gave her a thumbs-up signal as Jody breathed a sigh of relief. "Star looks good, doesn't he, Willie?" Mary asked nervously. "He's behaving himself too!"

"Well, he didn't do anything stupid, at least not yet," Willie replied dryly. "If you girls did your job grooming him, he should do alright in this class. Lots of competition though. They all look pretty clean and they're trotting right good. Except for the bay, of course."

Mary watched silently as the judge continued down the line of yearlings, questioning each handler. One of the colts refused to pick up his hoof at all, nipping his handler the minute she tried to run her hand down his leg. Another pinned his ears and kicked out when the judge patted his rump, barely missing the judge's leg. A few of the yearlings would square up perfectly for a minute but were too fidgety to hold the position for long. Star stood fairly still but occasionally would stomp his foot and try to rub his head up and down impatiently on Jody's arm. Mary crossed her fingers and prayed for the class to end before Star decided to "do something stupid." A moment later she got her wish, as the judge stepped back from the last yearling in line and jotted more notes on his clipboard.

"This concludes class number three, yearling grooming and showmanship," came the announcement at last. "If you are in the next class — class number four, yearling conformation — please remain in the ring after ribbons for class three are announced."

At this directive, Jody looked over at Willie, startled, while Mary's mouth opened in a big round *o*. "Remain in the ring? Willie, does he have to stay in there? Doesn't he get a break? He's getting impatient, and he's going to act up in a minute! Why do they do it that way?" Mary asked all in one breath.

"Well, it makes the show move along quicker that way, instead of havin' horses comin' and goin' so much, and I think they do it so they can see which of the yearlings can behave themselves the longest," Willie replied calmly.

"But, Willie…" Mary began, but her sentence was stopped short by the loudspeaker. "Please take your yearlings to the rail while we take a few moments to pin this class."

"See, they're goin' to let them walk around while they decide on the ribbons for grooming and showmanship," Willie explained. "That way they don't have to stand in one spot for so long."

"Willie, what's happening?" Jody whispered over the rail as she led Star past.

"They're going to give the ribbons for this class, and then you'll go right into the next one!" Mary answered before Willie had a chance. "Don't worry, you'll be fine!" she said encouragingly as Jody walked on.

It wasn't long before the voice boomed over the loudspeaker once again.

"I have the results of class number three, yearling grooming and showmanship. Please line up your yearlings. Line up facing the judge, please."

Mary jiggled nervously by the rail as Jody led Star back into line. A little girl with blonde pigtails skipped through the gate carrying a strip of cardboard that held the fluttering ribbons for first through sixth place. She took her place next to the judge and grinned at the competitors.

"Oh, Willie, this is too nerve-wracking!" Mary exclaimed as Jody tried again to square Star up. "Jody, don't worry about it now," she continued to the air. "The judging is all over!"

"If you are remaining in the ring for the next class," began the announcer, "please step forward and accept your ribbon, and when all placings have been called, hand it to someone outside the ring. In sixth place," the voice continued, "is number twenty-eight, Julianne Prettyman and Gold Bar."

Cheers erupted from a group of spectators as Julianne Prettyman happily stepped up with her palomino yearling to receive her prize.

"In fifth place, the team of Jessica Ferguson and Revlon." The woman standing next to Jody and Star proudly led her skewbald pinto yearling out of line and accepted her pink ribbon.

"Oh, Willie, do you think Star placed? He looked good, didn't he? Do you think he could have made the top four? Or maybe he didn't place at all, and he's in seventh or eighth place! Jody will be so upset!" Mary rambled, clutching the top rail of the ring with white-knuckled fingers.

"Hush now and listen to the announcement," Willie admonished. "I think you might hear Jody's name called yet."

"In fourth place, Brandon Gorin and Nellie's Nugget."

Brandon, the only boy in the ring, smiled broadly and trotted his flashy chestnut filly from the end of the line, halting neatly in front of the ribbon girl, who reached out and patted Nellie's Nugget on the shoulder as Brandon took the white ribbon from her grasp.

"Oh, Willie, I can't stand the suspense," Mary wailed. "And look, Jody is looking so nervous and Star is starting to stomp his foot like he always does when he's getting in an ornery mood," she continued in a panic.

"He'll be alright in a minute," Willie insisted. "He's just gettin' tired of standin' in one spot, just like the others. He's not the only one movin' around. Now will you hush up and listen?"

Mary clapped her hand over her mouth to quell her outbursts as the next announcement came. "And in third place, the team of Jody Stafford and Star of Wonder."

Mary's hand flew from her mouth as a happy shout emerged, and she jumped up and down with delight as Jody led Star forward and accepted her yellow ribbon. Willie grinned like a schoolboy in spite of himself, and putting two fingers in the corners of his mouth, he whistled loudly and then clapped right along with Mary. Jody, her head held high and grinning from ear to ear, led Star easily back into line and waited patiently for the top two ribbons to be announced before she trotted to ringside, so she could hand her ribbon over to Mary. But as she reached the fence, she held the ribbon briefly to her chest and looked first at Mary, and then Willie, as if making a decision. Then she reached over the top fence board and held the ribbon out to Willie.

"Can you hold this for me, Willie?" she asked quietly. "Thank you so much for all you've done for us."

Mary smiled at Jody as Willie wordlessly accepted the ribbon, nodding and tugging on his ear lobe. No one spoke until the next announcement came clearly over the loudspeaker.

"Again, our next class is class number four, yearling conformation. If you are not in this class, please exit the ring."

"Look, Willie, some of them are leaving! They must not be signed up for this class," Mary observed happily. "That means Star has a better chance!" But Mary's glee was short-lived as she watched three of the yearlings exit, because taking their place were four new yearlings, coming in through the gate just as the others went out.

"Willie, what's happening?" Jody whispered in a panic. "Why are there four more coming in?"

"Because there's four more entered in this class, that's why," Willie replied gruffly. "Those other three left because they were just entered in grooming and showmanship. Maybe because their yearlings don't have such good conformation. And look, the bay colt is leaving now too," Willie said, pointing at the rambunctious colt, who was trying to break away from his handler again as she led him to the gate. "Probably because he won't behave. So now it's nine, just like the last class."

"And that's your class," continued the announcer as the gate was officially closed. "Please take the rail with your yearlings."

"Jody, you should do even better this time!" Mary stage-whispered as Jody turned to walk Star along the rail. "Star's the prettiest colt in the whole class!"

Willie didn't speak but carefully folded the streamers of the cherished ribbon over and tucked it safely in the pocket of his shirt.

"Willie, what exactly is the judge looking for this time?" Mary asked. "Do you really think Star has a good chance?"

"We'll see," Willie said simply. "He's lookin' for how well Star's put together, the trueness to his breed, how well he moves, and just his overall appearance in general."

As Mary turned from Willie to watch the class, she noticed a man standing a slight distance away along the fence rail, closely observing Jody and Star as they walked along the rail. Then the man turned and looked at Willie in what Mary could only consider a glare. Mary continued watching the man, thinking that she must be imagining that he was only watching one colt in the class. But now it became painfully obvious that his gaze was locked firmly on Star alone.

"Willie," Mary began in a whisper, tugging on Willie's shirt sleeve. But before she could get her next word out, the man sidled over until he was standing close enough to hear whatever it was Mary was going to say next. Then he turned to Willie and glared again at such length that Willie noticed this time.

"How do?" Willie asked genially, turning to the man and tipping his hat.

"I'm alright. How are you?" the man replied in a less than friendly tone.

"Doin' just fine," Willie began, then he turned his attention back to the ring where the judge was asking the yearlings to line up.

"That your colt out there?" the man asked. "That piebald paint?"

"No, sir. Belongs to the girl showing him."

"You know anything about him?"

Something in his tone of voice made Willie turn and give the man his full attention. Mary was trying to watch the activity in the ring, where Jody was just at that moment being questioned by the judge, but she also turned and looked at the man questioningly. There was something about him that she definitely didn't like.

"Mary, you stay here in case Jody needs you. I'll be back," Willie said.

"But, but, Willie, what..."

"Stay here, I said," Willie commanded in his *you'd better mind me* voice. And then he walked away with the man, leaving Mary standing alone at ringside and feeling a sudden sense of dread.

9
The
Mysterious Man

MARY TRIED IN VAIN to pay attention to what was going on in the ring, but she could see Willie and the mysterious stranger standing a short distance away having a very animated conversation. The man pointed at Star several times, gesturing wildly and shaking his finger in Willie's face. Willie only shook his head and tugged repeatedly on his ear lobe. Mary was busting to hear what was being said but she knew she had to obey

Willie. And Jody would be really upset if she wasn't by the ring to support her.

"I have the results for class number four, yearling conformation," came the announcement from the loudspeaker.

"What, it's over already?" Mary asked herself. She had been so distracted by the nearby conversation that she had barely watched the class. She saw Jody glance her way and gave her the thumbs-up signal as the announcer continued.

"In sixth place, number thirty-nine, Sir Lancelot, shown by Megan Brebner."

Mary applauded politely but from the corner of her eye saw Willie and the man approaching the rail to watch the placings.

When the announcer bellowed, "fifth place goes to number twenty-eight, Julianne Prettyman and Bar of Gold," the group by the rail cheered even more loudly than in the previous class. Clearly pleased with winning yet another ribbon, the petite Miss Prettyman took the pink ribbon and waved to her family of fans.

"In fourth place is the team of Melissa Buckminster and Mr. Fritz." At the sound of her name, Melissa Buckminster squealed with delight. She had been in class number three and had not placed at all.

Mary stood by the rail biting her fingernails as each name was called. Without Willie to talk to, she had no outlet for her opinions. So she could only wait impatiently as her heart practically beat out of her chest in anticipation of the ribbon Star might get.

"Third place goes to Apollo, number sixty-two, shown today by Melissa Proctor."

Jody looked over at Mary and shook her head, certain that she had not placed in the ribbons. But Mary gave her the thumbs-up once again to demonstrate her loyalty, all the while keeping an eye on Willie and the stranger, who were watching the proceedings in silence.

"In second place is number fourteen, Ashley Eilers and Harmony." Ashley clapped her hands upon hearing her name called once again for second place, the same placing she had received in the grooming and showmanship class.

Mary jiggled uncontrollably, stomping her feet in place and swallowing hard to keep from crying out of sheer nervousness. It seemed forever before the announcer finally declared the name of the winner.

"And in first place in yearling conformation is number thirty-four, Jody Stafford and Star of Wonder."

Mary fairly shrieked when she heard Jody's name called. She wanted to run out into the ring and hug her best friend, but she satisfied herself with cheering at the top of her lungs when Jody stepped up to accept her ribbon. In her excitement, Mary forgot that Willie told her to stay put and ran over to be next to him at the rail.

"Willie! Can you believe it? We won! We won!" she shouted. Willie nodded and looked down at Mary with a forced smile that was not at all like him. And when Mary glanced over at the man still standing next to Willie, she saw him staring grimly out into the ring as Jody led Star to the gate. Then he turned abruptly and was gone.

"Jode! You did it! You did it!" Mary squealed the minute Jody and Star exited the ring. "See, you were shaking your head because you didn't think you placed, but I knew you did! I just *knew* it!" And she threw her arms around Jody with another squeal of delight while Star took one of Mary's brown curls in his teeth and pulled.

"Ow!" Mary yelped, trying to pull the section of hair from Star's mouth without leaving any behind. Jody dissolved into a fit of giggles and gave Star a great big pony hug around his neck.

"Oh my gosh, I can't believe it!" Jody said breathlessly. "Just think, Mary, this is only our second show, and we got another blue

*Star took one of Mary's brown curls
in his teeth and pulled.*

ribbon! First with Lady, and now with her baby!"

"Yes, we are definitely destined for stardom!" Mary laughed. "Willie, did you see Jody's ribbon?"

Mary had to turn to ask the question, because Willie was hobbling along behind the two girls and hadn't said a word.

"Yes, I seen it. Another one to add to your collection," he said half-heartedly.

"Willie, you were right about him being well put together. That's exactly what the judge said!" Jody continued, too happy to notice Willie's downturned face.

"Oh, what else did he say?" Mary prodded. "Did he say Star was the prettiest colt at the whole show? Because he is, you know. That's what I said. Oh, Jody, do you think we should enter some more classes? We know the judge likes Star. Maybe we could win some more ribbons!"

"No!" Willie spoke suddenly in a voice Mary and Jody had seldom heard from him.

"We've had enough for one day. Git Star over to the truck so we can git loaded up. If we hurry up, I can still make it home for milkin'."

"But, Willie, you don't have to do the milking any..." Jody began, but Mary poked her with an elbow before she could finish her sentence.

"OK, Willie, I was just getting carried away, I guess," Mary said sheepishly. "And Star's probably getting tired. We'll gather everything up while you get the truck ready."

Without another word, Willie turned and headed toward the old pickup truck. Mary and Jody stood for a minute and watched him, and then Jody turned and looked at Mary with a worried look on her face.

"What's wrong with Willie?" she asked. "He didn't even look happy about my ribbon, and he's hardly said a word!"

"I don't know, Jode. I don't know," Mary said ominously. "But I think we're going to find out."

10
Bad News

THE RIDE HOME to Lucky Foot Stable in Willie's pickup truck was much quieter than the ride to the show had been. Mary and Jody spoke softly to each other about the judge's comments, the good and bad qualities of the other yearlings at the show, and about how surprisingly good Star's behavior had been. But Willie was silent throughout the ride, lost in his own thoughts. Mary was dying to ask what those thoughts might be, but somehow she knew it wasn't the right time and that Willie would share them when he was ready.

Finnegan was waiting in the driveway when the trio arrived home, and he greeted them by barking ecstatically and turning in circles. Mary and Jody unloaded Star on the barn hill and took him to his stall, where they fawned over him and gave him pieces of carrot for a treat. Then they flew out to the big pasture, Finnegan nipping at their heels, to tell Lady and Gypsy all about the show. They found the two mares dozing under the weeping willow tree, switching flies with their tails.

"Lady! Look what Star won! You would have been so proud of your baby!" Jody yelled, running across the pasture waving Star's ribbons over her head. Lady, not the least bit impressed by this pronouncement, simply shook her head and began grazing. Jody hugged Lady around the neck and Mary gave Gypsy a kiss on the end of her nose. Then the girls flopped down on the soft grass beneath the tree as Finnegan rolled around on his back between them.

"Lad, the judge in the conformation class said that Star was going to grow into a fine looking horse," Jody continued, "and he asked me your name and the name of Star's sire."

"Did you tell him it was the Black Stallion?" Mary giggled.

"No, I was honest and said I didn't know his name. We never did find out anything about his father after that day we saw him at the show."

"Wait, Jode, did you say the judge said he would be a fine looking *horse?*" Mary asked.

"Yes, he asked me how tall he was, and I said fourteen hands, and he said he would probably grow at least another hand or so. So, Lady, he'll be taller than you!"

"Well, his father was huge, remember? Or maybe we just thought he looked huge because he was rearing up and being so mean," Mary recalled.

As she made the comment, Mary happened to look toward the pasture gate where she saw Willie gesturing for the girls to come over. Even from a distance, she could see he didn't look very happy.

"Uh-oh, Jode, Willie wants us for some reason," Mary said, bouncing up from the grass and pulling Jody up by the hand. "I wonder what's wrong."

"I was wondering what was wrong the whole way home," Jody said as they walked to the gate.

"Well, I don't know, but there was this man at the show that was watching you and Star and talking to Willie about something," Mary said hesitantly.

Jody stopped in her tracks and turned to Mary. "Watching me and Star? What do you mean?"

"Well, he was just watching you in the show and nobody else. And he didn't look too happy, and then he was talking to Willie for a long time, and Willie wouldn't let me listen…"

"Mary! Why didn't you tell me this before? What did he want? What did he look like?" Jody said in a sudden panic.

"Well, I didn't have a chance, and I don't know what he wanted, and why are you getting so upset before you know what it's all about?"

"I don't know, I just got a really bad feeling all of a sudden, that's all," Jody said. "We have to ask Willie!" And she took off at a trot toward the gate with Finnegan right beside her.

"Wait, Jody, I think Willie will tell us soon enough," Mary called after her. "You know he doesn't like it when we ask him questions. Let him tell us when he's ready," she continued wisely, picking up a trot herself to keep up with Jody.

By the time the girls reached the gate, Willie was tapping his foot impatiently and looking more unhappy than ever.

"Willie, what's wrong?" Jody asked, fearful of what the answer might be.

"Well, why don't you think a minute and tell *me* what's wrong?" Willie answered, stone-faced.

Jody looked at Mary and Mary looked back at Jody. "Um, well," Mary began, "um, weelll…" she continued for the lack of something better to say. Neither Mary nor Jody could think of what could be wrong.

"Um, well, nothin'" Willie snapped. "Was I s'posed to be the one to unload and put away all your show stuff, or was that s'posed to be you?"

"Oh my gosh, Willie, sorry!" Jody stammered. "We were so excited to see Lady and Gypsy when we got home, we forgot!"

"We'll clean it up right now, Willie! Sorry we left it all in the truck!" Mary said over her shoulder, already running to the barn hill where the truck was still parked.

"Wow, Willie is really mad," Jody whispered as they linked arms on their way up the hill.

"I know, and he usually isn't like that," Mary replied. "I mean, sometimes he yells at us for stuff, but it's not usually like that over something like this. Jody, something is bothering him."

The girls worked silently then, cleaning the straw out of the back of the pickup truck with a pitchfork and wheelbarrow and then sweeping it clean of every last bit of chaff. Jody grabbed her tack box from the front seat of the truck, while Mary chased after Finnegan to retrieve the unraveled tail wrap from his teeth. When the girls finally walked through the open barn doors of Lucky Foot Stable, Willie was waiting for them there.

"Put your stuff away and come sit down," Willie said grimly.

Mary and Jody were so taken aback by Willie's tone of voice they could only stand and stare at him.

"Come on now. I've got to go help Roy with the milking," Willie insisted.

Mary nervously wrapped the tail bandage around her hand while Jody carefully took the show supplies out of the tack box and placed them in their normal spot in the tack trunk. The girls instinctively moved more slowly than usual in an attempt to put off whatever it was that Willie was about to tell them. Finally, when they could stall no longer, they obediently sat together on a bale of hay. Finnegan lay at their feet, resting his chin on Mary's boots and whining softly as if he knew something was amiss. Colonel Sanders chose just that moment to come strutting into the stable, ruffling his feathers and clucking to himself. And even Star stopped munching on his pile of hay and hung his head over the stall door, nickering low in his throat as if to say, "Hey, why all the long faces?"

Willie took off his hat and pulled on his ear lobe. He looked up at the ceiling and cleared his throat. Then he smacked his hat against his knee and shook his head.

"Well, daggonit, there's no good way to say what I got to tell you," he said.

"What, Willie? What is it? You'll just have to tell us," Mary said, her voice quivering. Jody's heart was suddenly beating so loudly in her chest that she was sure it would drown out whatever it was Willie was about to say.

"Well, there was a man at the show today..." Willie began.

"I know, Willie, the man I saw looking at Star. What did he want?" Mary interrupted.

"Mare, let Willie talk, please," Jody squeaked.

"Well, that was the man that owned the stable where we took Lady to the horse show."

The girls looked at Willie openmouthed but didn't say a word.

"And he owns the stallion that is Star's sire. So when he saw Star, he just knew that he must be related somehow, because he's built just the same way and of course he's got the star on his forehead just like the stallion. But he knew that he hadn't bred the stallion to any mare that had a foal like Star."

Willie took off his hat and pulled on his ear lobe.

"Well, it wasn't our fault that Lady got in with the stallion that day. And we didn't even know she got pregnant until she had Star. It was a surprise!" Mary said indignantly.

"It wasn't a surprise to me," Willie reminded her.

"Willie, what does the man want?" Jody asked in a tiny voice, as the color completely drained from her face.

"Well," Willie said glumly, "it turns out that his stallion is one of the top-rated quarter horses in the country... not just the country, but the world. He's won championships all over the United States and overseas, too. Now the stallion's job is to sire championship foals, and the man gets top dollar for his breeding fees."

"So that's why Star is so gorgeous! His daddy is a champion! I knew it!" Mary said proudly, not yet realizing the gravity of the situation.

"Mary, the problem is that the man was pretty upset that Star had been born and he didn't even know about it. He needs to account for all of the stallion's foals, and he doesn't want any born without him getting the money that he asks for."

"So that means that people with mares pay him to breed the stallion to their mares so they can get nice foals, right?" Mary asked, while Jody sat wordlessly biting her fingernails.

"That's right. And he didn't get any money at all for his stallion fathering Star. Do you understand?"

The girls didn't speak for a minute. Mary stroked Finnegan's head and stared off into space. Then Jody finally found her voice.

"So, Willie, what does the man want?" she whispered.

Willie looked out the back door. He scratched the side of his head and rubbed a gnarly hand across his eyes. Then he looked at Jody and swallowed hard.

"He wants Star," he said.

11
No Hope?

Mary's mouth opened wide and a gut-wrenching wail came from deep within Jody when Willie finally made this terrible announcement. Finnegan whined helplessly and put his paw in Jody's lap, then he stood on his hind legs and licked the tears from her face. Colonel Sanders flapped his wings and hopped up on the bale next to her. Still she didn't speak. But Mary, when she finally found her voice, had plenty to say.

"But, Willie! He can't do that! He can't!

How could he just come and take Star away? He's half Lady's, isn't he?"

"I'm 'fraid he can," Willie said, turning his hat slowly in his hands. "He wanted to load him up and take him right then from the show, but when he saw how Jody was so taken with him and doin' such a good job showin' him, he said he'd give it a month."

"A month!" Mary exclaimed, while Jody sobbed with her hands over her face. "But, Willie, why did you tell him that Star was sired by that stallion? How could he prove it? Just because Star has the same star on his forehead doesn't mean…"

"Did you want me to lie to the man?" Willie asked sharply.

"Well, nooo… but, but, Willie, what are we going to do?" Mary wailed.

"What are we going to do about what?" Mrs. Morrow's voice came suddenly from the doorway. "How did Star baby do in the show?" she continued, then saw the stricken faces of Willie and the girls.

"What in the world is wrong?"

Mary jumped up from her seat on the bale and wrapped her arms around her mother's waist. "Mom, the worst thing in the whole world has happened!" she cried.

"What is it?" she asked, looking from Willie to Jody. "Jody, did you get hurt? Are you alright?"

"No, Mom, she's not hurt… well, yes, she is hurt. Her heart is hurt." Mary rubbed her eyes with her balled up fists and stepped back. "A horrible man at the show wants to take Star away! His stallion is Star's father, and he says Star should belong to him!"

Mary's mother looked at Willie questioningly. "Willie, is that true? Is that possible?"

"I'm 'fraid so, Mrs. Morrow," Willie answered. "Except that he's not such a horrible man; he just wants his champion stallion's progeny, that's all."

"But…" Mrs. Morrow began, then she sat down on the bale and put her arm around Jody.

"Oh honey, I am so sorry," she continued. "But, Willie, there must be something we can do!"

Just then it was Jody's father who came striding through the back door of Lucky Foot Stable. "Hey, guys… sorry I'm a little late picking you up… hey, what' going on? Jody, what's the matter? Did Star misbehave at the show?"

Jody had not been able to say a word through the lump in her throat, but when she saw her father, she jumped from the bale and threw her arms around him. "Oh, Daddy," she sobbed, her voice strangled by tears.

"Mr. Stafford, we got some bad news at the show," Willie explained wearily. "The man was there who owns Star's sire, and he was pretty mad about the fact that Lady was bred without him knowin' it. Turns out the stallion is a world champion quarter horse, and his owner wants the colt."

Mr. Stafford was silent, letting the information sink in before he spoke.

"Wants the colt? Can he do that?"

"As far as I know, he can," Willie repeated. "We can check into it, but he sounded pretty sure of himself. Now, he did say one thing…"

At this, Mary stopped crying and stared at Willie, and Jody turned from her father's grasp.

"What do you mean, Willie, he said one thing? What did he say? Something good?" Mary prodded.

"Well, not really. I wasn't gonna bring it up to you girls, but now that your parents are here, maybe it's something to think about… but I don't see how," Willie mumbled, wishing he hadn't brought up the matter at all.

"Willie, what is it? We'll do anything!" Jody cried.

"Well, he said if we could come up with the breeding fee — that's the money he gets from owners of mares who want to breed to his stallion," Willie explained for the benefit of the parents. "If we could pay that, then he'd let us keep the colt."

When she saw her father, she jumped from the bale and threw her arms around him. "Oh, Daddy."

"Willie! Why didn't you tell us that before? You made it sound like there was no hope!" Mary squealed. "We'll just have to work really hard and raise the fee!"

Willie and the girls' parents traded looks of grim understanding.

"How much is the breeding fee, Willie?" Mr. Stafford asked quietly.

"It's more than these girls could raise in a month of Sundays," Willie said matter-of-factly.

"But, Willie, we saved up almost forty dollars in one week when Mr. McMurray paid us to mind the roadside produce stand for him," Mary said proudly. "He said we sold more vegetables that week than he had the whole two weeks before. Maybe he'd let us mind it again."

Jody nodded hopefully at this suggestion, but she stopped when Willie spoke again.

"The breeding fee is over two thousand dollars," he said.

Mary opened her mouth but no sound

came out. Mr. Stafford looked at Mrs. Morrow without a word. Jody sat down on the bale and buried her face in Finnegan's neck. Willie rubbed his hand across his eyes and turned to Star, scratching him on that special spot on his shoulder. Then Mary looked at her mother pleadingly.

"Mom…" she began.

"Honey, you know we don't have any extra money. It's hard enough for me to pay the bills every month. I wish I could help, but…"

"Dad, what about that special fund you told me about? Can we use that?" Jody begged.

"I've just started to put aside some money for college, Jody. I am not going to touch that. And besides, it's not even close to what you'd need for this," Mr. Morrow said firmly.

"But I don't care about college!" Jody wailed. "I just want to keep Star! I can't give him up!"

"Willie, do you think Mr. McMurray would lend us the money?" Mary asked hopefully.

"You know Mr. McMurray just had that heart operation, Mary. That's why you were watching the stand for him, remember? He's got a lot of medical bills to pay. I heard him say the other day he was even thinkin' about sellin' the farm," Willie said, then he clamped his mouth tight, immediately regretting his words.

"Selling the farm?" Mary shouted in a sudden panic. "Willie, he's not selling the farm, is he? What would we do with Lady and Gypsy and Star if he sold the farm?"

"Now, thinkin' ain't doin'," Willie reassured Mary, although he wasn't feeling very reassured himself. "Now look, there's no use mopin' around here right now tryin' to figure this out. Star needs feedin' and turnin' out, and you girls need to go home and get a good night's sleep. Maybe tomorrow will look better, and we'll work on some ideas."

"Sleep? Willie, we won't be able to sleep. I'm never going to sleep again!" Mary declared.

Just at that moment, as if he knew he was

needed, Walter Pigeon sailed in through the back door of Lucky Foot Stable, hung in the air for a moment, and then landed squarely on the top of Jody's head. For the first time since Willie had delivered the bad news, Jody smiled through her tears and Mary even chuckled just a little.

"Willie's right, Jody," Mr. Stafford said gently. "Why don't you girls tend to Star and I'll wait for you in the car. Mary's still sleeping over at our house, isn't she?"

When Jody nodded, Walter went winging through the air and landed on his roost on the top board of Lady's stall. The Colonel strutted over and flapped up to join him there. Mary's mother walked out the back of the stable with Jody's father, murmuring low in conversation. Willie put on his hat and headed to the big white dairy barn to help finish the milking. It almost seemed like a normal afternoon at Lucky Foot Stable.

But it wasn't.

12
News
Travels Fast

CONTRARY TO MARY'S PREDICTION, both she and Jody fell asleep from exhaustion the moment their heads hit the pillows at Jody's house. When they awoke the next morning, they decided to clear their heads by taking a ride around the farm on Lady and Gypsy. They had been so busy in the previous months getting Star ready for the show that they had almost neglected their two ponies.

The ride to Lucky Foot Stable on their bikes was a silent one, each lost in her own thoughts and unwilling to share them. Jody was almost afraid to see Star with the possibility in the back of her mind that she might soon be parted from him. And Mary's brain was working overtime trying to come up with a plan to prevent just such a thing from happening.

As they pedaled up the gravel driveway of the farm, Star's cheerful whinny of greeting from the paddock gate made Jody burst into tears again.

"Oh, Mary, what are we going to do?" she whimpered as the girls parked their bikes just outside Lucky Foot.

"Now, first you've got to stop crying," Mary said cheerfully, trying to keep from crying herself. "We can't be morose. I looked that up, and it means, 'having a gloomy disposition.' Now, we're going to get Lady and Gypsy out of the pasture and get them ready to ride. We haven't even told them what's happening! Maybe if we talk about it some more, we'll get some ideas."

The last thing Jody wanted to do was talk about it, but she knew Mary was right.

So the girls made sure that Star had plenty of hay and water in his paddock, grabbed two lead ropes and a carrot, and ran out to the big pasture. There they found Lady and Gypsy, who were taking a long refreshing drink from the creek.

"Lady! Gypsy! We're here!" Mary called. "We know you've missed us!"

Lady and Gypsy responded by turning their heads in unison with water still dripping from their lips, and their ears pricked up at the sight of the girls galloping toward them. Mary and Jody slowed to a walk when they drew near the ponies and Mary broke the carrot into two equal pieces, handing one to Jody. At the sight of the carrots, the ponies nickered softly and trotted over to receive their treats.

"Just like old times," Mary murmured. Jody felt tears welling up once more in her eyes as Lady munched happily on the carrot.

She shook her head and wiped them away, determined not to be *morose*.

As they led Lady and Gypsy to Lucky Foot, the girls shared the whole story of the dilemma with them, and although the ponies could offer no solutions, of course, it did help a little to talk about it. Once inside the stable, the girls gave them a quick grooming job — a lick and a promise, as Mary put it. Then they bridled them up and were off on their tour of the farm.

"Let's ride up to the house and see if Mrs. McMurray is around," Mary suggested. "She's always in a cheery mood."

As the girls rode up the gravel lane, they saw up ahead a little towheaded boy playing in the sandbox in the tiny front yard of the house trailer where Annie lived with her family.

"Look, Mare, isn't that Heath out there all by himself?" Jody asked.

Just as the words escaped Jody's lips, Annie appeared in the doorway of the trailer with a bottle of juice in her hand.

"Mare, I don't want to be rude, but I don't really feel like talking to Annie right now," Jody whispered from the corner of her mouth. "Let's just trot on by and wave."

"I know, she might ask how Star's doing or something, and I don't really want to tell her about it just yet," Mary agreed.

So the girls clucked to the ponies and picked up a trot just as Annie came out into the yard to give Heath his juice.

"Hey, Annie, how're ya doin'?" Mary called out as they trotted past, waving merrily as if it was just another ordinary day.

"Hey," Annie replied and waved back. Then, as the girls continued trotting up the gravel drive, Annie yelled, "Sorry to hear about Star!"

Mary and Jody slowed to a walk and looked at each other in surprise. "Well, I guess she already knows," Mary said dryly. "I guess Willie must've told Annie's dad, and he must've told her. But now I *really* don't feel like talking about it."

"Hey, there's Mrs. McMurray!" Jody exclaimed, eager to get off the subject of Star.

Mrs. McMurray was busy hanging Mr. McMurray's overalls on the clothesline in the side yard of the big stone farmhouse, but she stopped and waved as Mary and Jody trotted up.

"Good morning, girls!" she called out in her lilting brogue. "Why, I haven't seen you riding for ages! And aren't the ponies looking fine!"

"Thanks, Mrs. McMurray. Willie says it's all the good grass they're getting in the pasture. We really appreciate Mr. McMurray letting them go out with the cows," Jody replied, hoping Mrs. McMurray would say it was OK for Star to go out there too. But Jody knew that decision was really Mr. McMurray's.

"Well, it's true. Grass is the best thing for horses or cows, either one," she nodded. "Now what's this I hear about the baby, then?" Mrs. McMurray put her hands on her hips and waited for a reply. Mary looked at Jody and could see her lips beginning to quiver, so she answered the question for her.

"Oh, it's awful, Mrs. McMurray. The man that owns Star's father wants to take Star away from us and we don't know what to do. But we're going to figure it out somehow," she added quickly.

"I know. Willie told Mr. McMurray all about it, and he told me. Now I wish there was something I could do to help, but you know Mr. McMurray hasn't been in the best of health…"

"Oh, we know, ma'am. Don't worry, we'll come up with something. We have a whole month, minus one day," Mary said, trying to sound confident for Jody's sake.

Mrs. McMurray turned to her basket of clothes, so the girls couldn't see that her lips were quivering as well. Then she straightened her back and turned to face them.

"Girls, don't forget that when God closes

*Mrs. McMurray was busy hanging overalls on
the clothesline in the side yard.*

a door, he opens a window," she said. "We must always remember that."

Mary and Jody nodded in unison. As they turned to ride on, Mrs. McMurray suddenly snapped her fingers.

"Now wait, I have an idea. Why don't you finish your ride and then come up to the house. I have a little job you can help with, and I can give you a little money for it too until you're better paid. It might start you on your way."

"OK! Thanks a lot, Mrs. McMurray. We'll be up in an hour or so," Mary assured her.

The kindly woman put her hands on her hips and watched as the girls rode down the driveway and onto the dirt path that led to the field of pines. She knew the scant amount of money she could pay them would do little to help with their dilemma, but she thought her little job would get their minds off their worries, and she thought it would be good for them to be near her if they wanted to talk. She stooped to get the last pair of Mr.

McMurray's overalls from the wicker basket, hung them on the line, and headed into the house to prepare the midday meal.

13
The Picking House

*J*T WAS JUST PAST NOON when Mrs. McMurray answered the knock on the double doors of the big stone farmhouse and ushered Mary and Jody into the bright blue and yellow kitchen.

"I'll just be a minute finishing up these dishes," she said, rinsing off the last plate and putting it in the drying rack on the drainboard. "How was your ride then?"

"Oh, it was so nice," Jody sighed. "We

saw a fox in the pine field, and he just sat and looked at us. He didn't even run away!"

"And then we practiced cantering in and out in a serpentine around the littlest trees at the far end. Lady and Gypsy are so good at that! Our legs never even got scratched by the pine needles!" Mary added proudly.

"Well, I'm glad you had a good time. Are you ready for a little work?" Mrs. McMurray asked, wiping her hands on her apron.

"Sure we are!" Mary announced. "What are we going to do?"

"Well, we're going out to the picking house to dress some chickens for market. Mr. McMurray got a big order this week, so we need a few extra hands. Roy and Jimmy are already out there. Now, if you'll wait just a minute, I'll get my singeing pan."

Mary and Jody looked at each other wide-eyed, completely lost by what Mrs. McMurray had just said.

"Why do we have to dress up the chickens?" Jody wondered out loud. "Are they going to sell them with clothes on?"

"Maybe Mr. McMurray sells chickens to the carnival. Have you ever seen those chickens that dance and play tic-tac-toe and stuff? Maybe he's dressing them up for that," Mary guessed.

"But what's a singeing pan?" Jody asked.

"And I don't even know where the picking house is," Mary added, baffled by all the new terms and wondering why, in all their years at the farm, they had never heard them before.

"Well, come on then, girls. Follow me," Mrs. McMurray instructed, striding out the door with a metal pan that looked like it was previously used for canned ham. Mary and Jody followed obediently through the door and around the back of the house where a small cinder block building sat at the corner of the chicken yard. Outside the building was a huge black pot with a fire going under it and steam wafting from the top. When Mary and Jody passed by the pot, they saw that the water was close to boiling inside. Near the pot was a long metal pole hanging lengthwise between the lower branches of two mimosa trees. From the pole there hung five or six lengths of baler twine with a loop at each end. Mary and Jody, still dutifully following Mrs. McMurray, almost tripped over each other as they stared at all the strange apparatus. Then they entered the picking house.

There in the little building were Mr. Mc-Murray, Annie's father, and her brother. They all sat silently hunched over the task at hand, which was definitely not putting clothes on chickens. In fact, the newly deceased chickens were in various stages of nakedness, in the process of having their feathers plucked out. These were white-feathered birds, unlike the Rhode Island Red hens in the egg-laying house. Mary and Jody gasped in unison at the sight before them. Now they understood why the little building was called the picking house.

"But, but, but… Mrs. McMurray, I thought you said we were going to dress up the chickens," Mary sputtered.

"Dress up…?" Mrs. McMurray began, and then she stifled a grin. "Oh no, Mary — I said we were going to *dress* the chickens; that means get them ready for market, for people to eat. Now, you like chicken, don't you?"

"I used to," Mary said, putting her hand over her mouth. Jody simply stared speechlessly at the plucking process.

"Um, Mrs. McMurray, is there another job you might like us to do?" Mary asked sweetly. "We could go gather the eggs for you…" she suggested, turning in unison with Jody to flee the premises as quickly and quietly as possible.

"*Girls.*"

The word was practically spat from Jimmy's mouth. "Shoulda known better than to ask *girls* to do a job like this. They're just

There in the little building sat Mr. McMurray,
Annie's father, and her brother.

chickens themselves," he continued, shaking his head but never looking up from the bird he was plucking.

Mary and Jody stopped in their tracks and looked at each other in shock. They had seen Jimmy around the farm, getting the cows in for milking or helping his father repair farm equipment. They had commented on how he looked so different from Annie with his dark hair and broad shoulders. But they had never actually heard him speak. And they definitely didn't take kindly to the first words they had heard him say.

"Jimmy, hush," Roy admonished his son. Jimmy just shook his head and continued plucking. But the challenge was too much for Mary.

"Mrs. McMurray, I think we can help you with this after all," she offered bravely. "Now, what do we do first?"

"But, Mare..." Jody squeaked, pinching the sleeve of Mary's shirt.

"Jody, Jody, it's fine. The chickens are… are… no longer with us, so they don't feel a thing. And besides, the feathers have to be taken out, or there's no way you could eat the chicken. Right, Mrs. McMurray?"

"Yes, that's right, Mary," Mrs. McMurray agreed solemnly. "And after the feathers are picked out, the innards have to be taken out as well. Now we don't need help so much with that part as Jimmy and Roy are both here, but we could use a couple of extra hands picking."

Jody's mouth flew open at the thought of "taking out the innards," but Mary was not to be outdone by Jimmy. "Well, now, Mrs. Mc-Murray, if you do need help with those in-nards, we'll be here," Mary said confidently.

"What do you mean, we?" Jody whispered in Mary's ear. "I'm not doing that!"

Mrs. McMurray turned away so the girls couldn't see her stifling a grin. "Now just wait here by the table, girls. It looks like Mr. McMurray is getting a chicken ready for you," she said, bustling out the door toward the steaming black kettle. Jody grimaced. Through the open door she saw Mr. Mc-Murray holding a chicken by the feet and dipping it several times into the pot.

"Oh, Mary, do they drown the poor chickens?" Jody sputtered. "Is that how they do it?"

Jimmy glared at Jody in disbelief. "Don't you know anything?" he growled. "The chickens are already dead when he dips them. The hot water loosens up the feathers, so you can pull them out easier."

"Girls, the chickens are put to sleep very fast so they don't feel anything," Jimmy's father began kindly. "Now, what Mr. McMurray does is…"

"Ohhh, that's OK, Mr. Mooney. You don't have to explain it or anything," Jody interrupted while Jimmy rolled his eyes.

Mary and Jody were ready at the long oilcloth-covered table when Mrs. McMurray returned with the steaming chicken. When she plopped it down in front of the girls,

Jody stepped back in dismay while Mary leaned forward curiously to get a closer look. Mrs. McMurray put both hands on the sodden breast feathers and began vigorously pulling them backward until they came out in handfuls.

"Now, you see, the feathers come out easily when they are dipped in the hot water first," she explained. "After we get the main feathers out of the breast and wings, then you can sit down and pluck the smaller ones. And then we put a little fire in the singeing pan to singe off the tiny hair-like ones," she instructed briskly. "Now, who's ready to give it a try?"

"I am!" Mary raised her hand courageously.

Jody glanced sideways at the lifeless bird and took another step back. "I'll watch you first," she said.

Secretly hoping Jimmy was watching, Mary put her hands on the breast of the chicken just as Mrs. McMurray had and swept the rest of the small breast feathers from the yellow breast. Then she took the longer wing feathers in hand and pulled them out one by one.

"See, Jode, nothin' to it," she crowed.

"What have we got here then?" Mr. McMurray boomed, coming through the door with another chicken ready to be plucked. "Brand new chicken pickers?"

"Yes, sir, Mr. McMurray. It's not so bad when you get used to it," Mary said, turning the chicken over so she could get to the feathers on the back.

"Hmmph," Jimmy snorted from his seat. He handed the chicken he had been plucking to Mrs. McMurray for singeing and stood to work on the one Mr. McMurray had just set on the table.

"Hey, it's Jody's turn with that one!" Mary admonished, looking up at Jimmy, who was really quite a bit taller up close than she had expected.

"She's not gonna do it," he smirked.

"Oh yes, I am," Jody declared, pushing her way between Jimmy and Mary and taking command of the breast feathers. "I can do it just as well as you can."

Mr. and Mrs. McMurray exchanged amused glances with Mr. Mooney, and then it was all silence in the picking house, as they each attended to the task at hand. Jimmy stood by and watched Jody with grudging respect as she enthusiastically took to the job of plucking the breast feathers, even offering his assistance when it came time to pull out the larger wing feathers.

"Move your hand down closer to the chicken's body and pull them out from the base instead of grabbing them by the end," he suggested. "They come out easier that way, and you don't break them off."

"OK, thanks," Jody murmured, forgetting her resentment and concentrating on doing the job just so. Mary was already seated with a burlap feed bag on her lap, working on the smaller feathers of her chicken, and Mrs.

McMurray was carefully passing a plucked bird over the small flame in the singeing pan, burning off the last of the tiny hair-like feathers.

It was almost time for milking when the picking crew finished the last of the poultry that had been ordered for market. Jimmy and Roy left to help Willie get the cows into the barnyard, and Mary and Jody stayed behind to assist Mrs. McMurray with the sweeping of all the wayward feathers from the picking house floor.

"Now, we'll finish up after milking, but as I said, you girls don't have to help with that part," Mrs. McMurray said generously, not mentioning again exactly what that part would be. Then another thought occurred to her.

"You know, we do have a few extra chickens that haven't been ordered for market," she said. "Should I call your parents and tell them? Wouldn't you like some fresh chicken for dinner tonight?"

"No!" Mary and Jody shouted in unison.

"I mean, thanks, Mrs. McMurray, but I don't think I could eat chicken right now," Mary said sheepishly.

"Me either," Jodi agreed. "It's different when it comes from the grocery store and you don't know it personally."

This time Mrs. McMurray didn't even try to hide her amusement. "OK, girls, I understand," she laughed. "Now come on up to the house and I'll pay you for your labor. I know it won't help your predicament much, but it's a little something, anyway."

The girls sighed as they followed Mrs. McMurray to the big stone house. They had been so involved in learning the new skill of chicken plucking that they had almost forgotten about the crisis with Star. And that was just what Mrs. McMurray had intended.

14
The Visitor

THE NEXT MORNING found Mary and Jody straddling the lowest and thickest branch of the horse chestnut tree in the side yard of the big stone farmhouse, shelling corn off of the cob by hand for the Muscovy ducks that roamed freely on the property. The squatty white ducks fought each other greedily for the hard kernels of corn dropping from the tree, swallowing them whole and pecking the ground for more. The girls would normally be giggling at the antics of the funny-looking fowl, but this morning they were too lost in thoughts of Star and the dreadful possibility of losing him. Neither of them wanted to be the first to bring up the subject, so they sat apathetically loosening the corn from the cob with their thumbs and watching in silence as each yellow kernel dropped to the ground.

The silence was suddenly interrupted by the sound of a car's tires crunching on the gravel of the long farm lane. Mary and Jody looked up to see a small blue sedan pull up in the driveway of the farmhouse and a man with a clipboard in his hand emerge and knock on the door.

"They're not home," Mary said quietly so that only Jody could hear. "They're off to market to sell naked chickens."

Jody giggled in spite of herself as they continued to watch the man. He knocked once more and then turned and got back in his car. But rather than driving out the lane, he steered toward the house trailer where the Mooneys lived. Mary and Jody peered through the leaves of the horse chestnut tree, as the man got out of his car once more and spoke to Annie, who was out in the front yard playing with Heath. Annie disappeared into the trailer and soon reappeared with her father, who began a long conversation with the man. Mary and Jody watched him gesture and point at various spots around the farm, first at the farmhouse, and then the barn, and finally at Lucky Foot Stable.

"What in the world do you think he wants?" Jody asked, throwing her empty corncob to the ground, where the Muscovys fought over it until they realized there was no corn left.

"I don't know. Maybe he's a salesman. Willie said a man stopped by last week and wanted to paint the barn, and another one came that wanted to put a new roof on. Mr. McMurray's always turning them away," Mary answered indifferently. "Come on, let's go down to Lucky Foot and bring Star in and groom him. Maybe we should put his saddle and bridle on and walk him around the farm. We're going to have to start putting some of our weight on him soon to get him used to the feel of it."

Jody didn't reply but tears once again sprang to her eyes. *Maybe Star won't be around long enough to start putting our weight on him. What are we going to do?*

The girls swung down together from the thick branch of the tree, scattering ducks every which way, and linked arms on their way to the stable. As they passed the house trailer, the man with the clipboard was walking toward the big white dairy barn with Mr. Mooney, and Annie and Heath were nowhere to be seen.

"Wow, Mr. Mooney is spending a lot of time with that man. Mr. McMurray usually just sends them on their way," Mary observed.

"Mare, maybe he wants to buy the farm!" Jody cried in a sudden panic. "Willie said Mr. McMurray was thinking about selling it!"

"Well, if he wanted to buy the farm, he would have to talk to Mr. McMurray, not Mr. Mooney," Mary replied matter-of-factly. "Let's not worry about that until we know what it's all about. We have other things to worry about, you know."

This was the first reference to the trouble with Star, and still Jody could not bring herself to talk about it. Oh, if only not talking about it would make it go away!

Mary and Jody entered the cool stillness of Lucky Foot and were calmed by the sight of Finnegan sleeping peacefully in a spot of sun just inside the stable doors and Colonel Sanders strutting around pecking at imaginary pieces of grain on the dirt floor. They went silently to the Dutch doors leading to the paddock and leaned over. Star was napping on his feet at the far end, the tip of his nose almost touching the ground.

"Star!" Jody called softly. "Wake up, little guy!"

Now it was Mary's turn to get a lump in

her throat as Star raised his head and nickered softly at the sight of the two girls.

"Hey, buddy, come on over," Jody called again. Star stretched himself fore and aft like a dog, shook his head and yawned, then strolled over to where Mary and Jody waited with hands outstretched. He sniffed both of their hands in turn, looking for treats and then snorting wetly in their faces. Mary and Jody giggled through their tears and opened the bottom of the Dutch door to lead him in for grooming. When Mary turned to open his stall door, Annie was standing in the middle of the stable aisle.

"Hi," she said.

"Geez, Annie, you scared me to death!" Mary yelped. "What are you doing here?"

"Well, that's not a very nice greeting," Annie commented, peering over the top of her horn-rimmed glasses. "Can't I come visit once in a while?"

"Sure you can, Annie," Jody answered,

leading Star into his stall. "We just didn't see you there, that's all. You surprised us."

Annie didn't reply, but she leaned over the top board of Star's stall and held her hand out to him. Star instantly began licking her palm. Mary and Jody looked at each other, a little peeved at the effect Annie seemed to have on all members of the animal kingdom.

"So, how's he doing, anyway?" she asked, continuing to give Star a taste of her palm.

"He's doing fine," Mary said shortly.

"But we're not," Jody added glumly. Since Annie already knew about the dilemma, Jody figured it was OK to bring it up. And somehow it seemed easier for Jody to talk about it with Annie around instead of with just Mary. "We have less than a month to figure it out, and we don't know what to do."

"Hmmph," Annie replied, never turning away from Star. The only sound in the stable was a gentle snore coming from the sleeping

Finnegan and the low intermittent cluck of Colonel Sanders who was still searching for stray pieces of grain.

Then Annie said, "I know what you can do."

Mary and Jody looked at Annie, then at each other. Knowing that Mary would slowly go crazy trying to get information from Annie, Jody took the next step.

"Well, OK, Annie. What can we do?" she asked.

"Well, there was a man here today," Annie began.

"We know; we saw him. So what's that got to do with Star?" Mary asked, already impatient with Annie's reticence.

"He was looking for Mr. McMurray, but he wasn't home," Annie said.

"We know; we saw him go down and talk to your dad. What did he want?" Jody asked patiently.

"Well, he wanted to look around the farm. He's looking for a specific place,"

Annie continued, turning from Star for the first time to face the girls.

"A specific place for what?" Mary almost shouted, wanting to shake Annie to get the words out of her more quickly.

"A movie," Annie said.

Mary and Jody stared at Annie speechlessly. Finnegan let out a particularly loud snore. Then Mary found her voice, as she always did.

"What kind of movie?" she asked breathlessly.

"I'm not sure, exactly. But the man said he was a location scout, and he needs a dairy farm for a movie, and there's going to be horses in it too, and he wants Willie."

"Willie? Why does he want Willie?" Jody sputtered.

"Well, him and my dad were talking, and my dad told him that Willie works here, and what with Willie being a famous wrangler and all..."

Mary and Jody looked at each other

without a word. Then they turned back to Annie.

"Annie, what do you mean, a famous wrangler? What do you mean by that?" Mary demanded.

"We didn't know the whole story either, though Willie had told my dad some of it. But when my dad told the man Willie's whole name, the man got real excited and said, 'Will Riggins works here? Do you know who he is? Why, he worked with some of the best in the business in his day. He was in demand on all the western movie sets to wrangle the horses and help the actors with their riding. We could sure use him on this!'"

Mary's mouth opened wide and she grabbed Jody's arm. "Jode! This all makes sense!" she said, wide-eyed. "Do you remember the time we went in Willie's house to ask him where Star was, and we saw that picture of him with John Wayne? We never did ask him about that! He must've worked with John Wayne and who knows who else?

Oh my gosh! Willie's famous! And he can work on this movie and they'll pay him, and he can use the money to save Star!"

"That's what I thought," Annie said, deadpan.

"But, Mary, even if they do use the farm for the movie and Willie gets a job, it's his money. We can't ask him to use it for Star," Jody cried.

Mary clamped her mouth shut tight and thought for a minute. "Well, no, we can't. But I bet Willie will want to do it! I bet he'll come up with the idea all on his own."

Then she turned to Annie and grabbed *her* arm. "Annie! Is that man still here?" she asked breathlessly.

"I think so. My dad took him around the back of the barn to talk to Willie," she said.

Before Annie could say another word, Mary and Jody had flown out the door of Lucky Foot Stable and were headed for the big white dairy barn. Finnegan raised his head and whined once, but then he jumped up too and took off after them as fast as he could go.

Mary and Jody fairly flew to the dairy barn with Finnegan nipping at their heels. But when they rounded the corner and saw Willie and Mr. Mooney standing on the barn hill in front of the big barn doors talking to the man with the clipboard, Mary grabbed Jody's arm and they stopped in their tracks. Then, as if out for a leisurely roam around the farm, they nonchalantly strolled up the hill toward the trio, stopping about ten feet from where the men were engaged in serious conversation. Willie held up his hand to the men and turned to the waiting girls with eyebrows raised.

"Um, Willie," Mary said, smiling sweetly at the stranger. "Um, excuse us for interrupting, but we were just wondering, just wondering if... if..."

"We were just wondering if you wanted us

to help feed the calves today," Jody continued, smiling just as sweetly.

"Feed the calves? Since when do you volunteer for that job?" Willie asked, narrowing his eyes suspiciously at the girls.

"Well, who do we have here, Will?" asked the man, smiling with his hand outstretched. "Good afternoon, girls. I'm Ted Crowley with Eyepatch Productions." Ted Crowley shook hands with both girls and turned back to Willie. "Are these your barn helpers?"

"I reckon you could call them that," Willie muttered. "Now, why don't you girls go… "

"You know, we're going to need girls just about this age for the film," the wonderful Mr. Ted Crowley interrupted. "There are several scenes where the lead character is teaching riding lessons, and she'll need some students on horseback. Would you girls be interested in helping us out with that?"

"Film? There's going to be a film?" Mary asked innocently. "You mean like a movie?"

Ted Crowley shook hands with both girls and
turned back to Willie.

"Well, we hope so. We've been looking for a dairy farm just about like this one for our movie, and we're hoping Mr. McMurray will agree to it. And just by dumb luck, we found Will here, who we're hoping will agree to accept the job of head wrangler."

"Head wrangler!" Jody said, wide-eyed. "Does Willie know how to do that?"

"Does he know how to do it?" Mr. Crowley asked incredulously. "Well, I guess he does! Hasn't he ever told you…"

"Now, now, why don't you girls go on around the barn?" Willie interrupted, tugging vigorously on his ear lobe. "I guess I do need some help feedin' those calves. Why don't you go on now and get started?"

"But, Willie, it's only noontime, and the calves don't get fed until three o'clock," Mary grinned. "We have lots of time to talk to Mr. Crowley!"

Mr. Mooney stole an amused look at Willie, who had taken off his hat and was scratching the side of his head in agitation.

"Well, Mr. Crowley doesn't have lots of time to talk to you," Willie said pointedly. "He's got things to do. Now get on around the barn and I'll be around shortly."

In his last sentence, Mary and Jody recognized Willie's *you'd better mind me* voice. They turned to head down the barn hill, but not before Mary took the opportunity to get in a parting shot.

"It was very nice to meet you, Mr. Crowley, and we sure would be interested in helping you out with those riding scenes in your movie," she piped.

Willie shook his head, Mr. Mooney grinned, and Mr. Crowley smiled and waved good-bye to the girls. When Mary and Jody reached the corner of the barn where the men could no longer see them, they took off at a gallop once again with Finnegan yipping happily beside them to share with Lady and Gypsy the astounding news of their imminent film stardom.

And to plan the salvation of Star.

15
Willie to the Rescue

ON THEIR JOYFUL SPRINT back to Lucky Foot, Mary and Jody slowed down long enough to stop in at the big pasture where they found Lady and Gypsy grazing peacefully near the gate.

"Lady! Gypsy! We're going to be movie stars!" Mary called gleefully to the ponies, who responded by lifting their muzzles just inches from the grass. "And even better, we're going to keep Star!"

"Mary, don't say that yet!" Jody said

sternly. "We don't know for sure, and I can't get my hopes up, because it will be even worse if it doesn't happen."

"Sorry, Jode, but I just think it will. I mean, this is so perfect! Mr. McMurray will get some money for letting them use the farm, and then he won't have to sell it, and Willie will get paid for being the wrangler, and we might even get paid for being in the riding scenes, and then we'll have enough money to pay for the breeding fee! Do you think they'll pay us for riding in the movie?"

"I don't know, Mare, I've never been in a movie before! And maybe Mr. McMurray won't want them to use the farm. You know how protective he is of the cows and everything. And Willie might think he's getting too old to be the wrangler. What exactly does a wrangler do anyway? And what is a head wrangler? It sounds like he wrangles people's heads or something," Jody said despondently.

"Now, stop being so pessimistic. Let's go

to Lucky Foot and tell Star what's happening, and we'll make a plan."

"How can we make a plan when we don't know what's happening?" Jody asked, still refusing to believe that something so wonderful could actually be forthcoming.

When the girls entered Lucky Foot Stable with Finnegan trotting along behind, Mary could hardly contain herself long enough to reach Star's stall where he was busy munching on his pile of hay. "Star!" Mary yelled. "You'll never guess what…"

Mary was abruptly stopped mid-sentence by Jody's hand clapped over her mouth. "Mare, I'm not kidding. We are not going to talk about this any more until we know it's true," she commanded. "I'm not going to move my hand until you nod your head and promise."

Mary looked at Jody beseechingly with her big green eyes, but Jody only stared back sternly, actually tightening the grip on Mary's mouth. Finally, Mary nodded slowly up and down and held up her right hand in the symbol of a solemn vow.

"Good," Jody said quietly, dropping her hand to her side. "Now, we are going to turn Star out in the paddock and do our chores around the stable and wait for Willie. He said he would be around soon, and he'll tell us what's really going on."

Mary picked up the broom from its place in the corner and silently began sweeping the packed dirt floor. After Jody led Star out to the paddock, she took a clean hard brush from her tack trunk and unclipped the half-empty water bucket from the inside post of his stall. Carrying the bucket to the back of the stable, she took it in both hands and flung the remaining water out the doors.

"Hey! Watch that!"

Jody's father just happened to be entering Lucky Foot Stable at that unfortunate moment. Luckily, the water barely reached him, just splashing a little on his work boots and the leg of his jeans.

"Daddy! What are you doing here?" Jody cried, dropping her bucket in surprise.

"Well, I just finished up that trim work I've been doing in the farmhouse. I thought it would be a good day, since the McMurray's were off to market. They got home just as I was cleaning up."

Mr. Stafford offered his carpentry services to Mr. McMurray in return for boarding Lady and Star. Whenever he had a spare moment from his own work, there was always something to be done around the farm.

"Oh Dad, you won't believe it! We might have some good news!" Jody cried, pulling her dad by the hand into the stable.

"Ahem!" Mary coughed noisily in Jody's direction, shooting her a look of warning.

"Oh, but we really can't talk about it yet," Jody said sheepishly. "Not until Willie gets here."

"I'm here," Willie said from the doorway. "How do, Mr. Stafford?"

"Good, Willie, thank you. I hear you have some good news for the girls?"

Willie tugged on his ear lobe and looked from one girl to the other. "Well, maybe it is and maybe it isn't. Depends."

"Depends on what, Willie?" Mary cried, unable to hold her tongue any longer.

"Depends on how much damage the film crew does to the ground here. If they mess it up too bad, we might wish we'd never said they could do it."

Mary and Jody stared at Willie, trying to absorb the meaning of what he had just said. It was Jody who finally found her voice.

"What do you mean, Willie? Did Mr. McMurray say they could do it?" she squeaked.

"Well, Mr. McMurray got home just as the scout was leavin'," Willie explained. "He laid out the idea to him, and it sounds like it might go through."

Mary and Jody squealed and joined hands, jumping up and down and turning in circles while Finnegan joined in, yipping excitedly. Mr. Stafford looked on, completely baffled by all the commotion.

"I did see that man talking to Mr. McMurray on my way down here," he said. "What's this all about, Willie?"

"Oh, Dad, that man was here looking for a dairy farm they could use to make a movie…" Jody began.

"And he wants Willie to be the head wrangler, and he wants us to ride in a riding lesson, and oh my gosh, I bet he might want to use Lady and Gypsy too, and…" Mary went on.

"And then Mr. McMurray won't have to sell the farm, and Willie can use the money he makes as a wrangler to save Star…" Jody cried. Then she stopped and clapped her hand over her own mouth at the words she had just let fly.

Jody's father looked at Willie, then sternly at Jody. "Jody, stop right now. If what you're saying is really true, and Willie does work

*Mary and Jody squealed and joined hands, jumping
up and down and turning in circles.*

on the film, that's his money, not yours. Now, I think you owe him an apology."

"I'm sorry, Willie," Jody said, hanging her head. "I know it's not my money. We just got carried away, hoping we could save Star. But, Dad, maybe we'll get paid for being in the movie too and maybe we could use that money for the breeding fee."

Willie took off his hat and scratched the side of his head, then he rubbed his gnarly hand across his eyes before he spoke. "Jody, you will get paid for riding in the movie. But it won't be very much. It won't be enough to pay for the breeding fee."

Jody's father patted her on the back sympathetically. Mary sat silently on a bale and looked up at Willie expectantly.

"But now look. I wasn't expectin' anything like this to happen, especially at my age," Willie said quietly. "And I always figure things happen for a reason. Now, Mr. Stafford, I don't have any family left, and I sure ain't plannin' on goin' out and buyin' any real estate at this time in my life. I'm pretty happy with the way things are."

Mary stroked Finnegan's head and tried not to breathe. She looked back and forth between Jody and Willie as a faint smile played around her lips.

"And I guess I care just about as much for that ornery bugger as anybody else," Willie continued. "I already made up my mind that if these girls need that money to keep him around, I'd be happy to help out."

Mary tearfully hugged Finnegan around his neck. She was speechless for one of the only times in her life. Mr. Stafford put his arm around Jody and squeezed, then he held out his hand to Willie.

"Thank you, sir," he said. "We definitely owe you one for this."

Jody, choking back a sob, looked at Willie with tears welling up in her eyes and simply put her arms around him in a grateful embrace.

"Now, now, don't get all weepy on me,"

Willie said gruffly. "There's work to be done. Didn't you girls say you were goin' to feed those calves for me today?"

"We did, Willie. But, but… I think there is still a problem," Mary said worriedly. "We only have a month to come up with the money! When does the movie start filming? Will we have enough time?"

"They want to start pretty much right away, since they want to be done by the end of the summer. And I think I already took care of the money part. Mr. Crowley is going to talk to the production company, but he's fairly sure they can give me an advance, since he thinks they'll be real excited to have me as the wrangler, for some reason," Willie said modestly.

Jody smiled through her tears and looked up at her father. "Dad, did you know that Willie was a famous wrangler? He worked in all the movies when he was younger, getting the horses and even the actors ready for their scenes. And in this movie, he's going to be the *head* wrangler. Willie, what is the head wrangler anyway?"

For one of the few times since the girls had known him, Willie laughed out loud.

"Head wrangler just means I'm in charge. If they need any other people to work with the horses or other livestock, I'll be tellin' them what to do."

The girls absorbed this information in silence, but they looked at Willie with a new respect — even greater than that which they already had for him.

"Now, enough of this foolishness. Them calves'll be bawlin' their heads off pretty soon for lack of food," Willie said, trying to sound grumpy.

"I think I'm going to write a poem about this," Jody announced.

"Well, maybe you should write lots of poems and put them in a book, and we could sell it and get rich, and then we wouldn't have to use Willie's or our movie money to save Star," Mary suggested.

"Good plan!" Jody laughed. "Oh my gosh, speaking of Star, we haven't even told him what's going on yet!"

"Well, you wouldn't let me until we knew for sure, remember?"

Jody smiled, and while her father and Willie walked out the back door of Lucky Foot Stable together, Mary and Jody linked arms and trotted out to the paddock to share with Star the wonderful news of how Willie had once again come to the rescue.

Glossary of Horse Terms

bale — In stable terms, a bale is a closely packed bundle of either hay or straw (see definitions) measuring about two by three feet, weighing about forty pounds and tied with two strings lengthwise. When the strings are cut, the bale can be shaken loose and either fed, in the case of hay, or used for stall bedding, in the case of straw.

baling twine — The term used for the thick yellow string that is tied around a bale.

bank barn — A barn that is built into the side of a hill so that the hill forms a "ramp" leading into the upper part of the barn, where hay and straw may be stored; the bottom floor of the barn is used for milking the cows if it is a dairy barn, or it may have stalls for the purpose of sheltering other animals.

barn swallow — A small, blue-black bird with a rusty-colored breast and throat and forked tail; found all over North America and Europe, these friendly birds like to build their nests in barns and eat insects.

barrel — The middle section of the body of a horse or pony between the shoulder and the flank.

bay — A common color seen in horses and ponies. The body is reddish-brown with black mane, tail, and lower legs

bit — The metal piece on the bridle inserted

into the mouth of a horse that provides communication between the rider and horse.

bridle — The leather headgear with a metal bit that is placed on the head of a horse to enable the rider to control the horse.

bridle path — A section of mane about an inch wide behind the ears that is trimmed short to allow the crown piece of the bridle to lie flat and fit more comfortably.

cannon bone — A bone in the leg of the horse or pony running from the knee or hock to the ankle.

cantankerous — ill-mannered or quarrelsome.

canter — A three-beat gait of the horse, which could be called a "collected gallop." It is slightly faster and not so "bouncy" as a trot.

chaff — the seed covering separated from the seed when grain is threshed.

chestnut — A common color found in horses and ponies. The coat is basically red, in varying shades on different horses. The mane and tail are the same color as the body.

cluck — The "clicking" sound a rider or driver makes from the corner of the mouth to urge a horse forward. Also the sound a chicken makes when communicating.

corncob — The inner segment of an ear of corn to which the corn kernels are attached. The horse eats the kernels but not the cob.

crop — A short, leather riding whip carried by the rider and used lightly to encourage the horse to move forward.

crosstie — The method of tying a horse

squarely in the aisle or stall by which a rope is clipped to both sides of the halter. When a horse is crosstied, he cannot move away from the rider during grooming and saddling.

dam — the mother of a horse or pony.

dismount — The action of getting down from a horse and onto the ground.

dock — The bone in the horse's tail, which is formed of the lowest vertebrae of the spine.

Dutch door — A door divided horizontally in the middle so that the two sections can be opened separately.

eaves — The overhanging lower edge of a roof.

fetlock — The part of the lower leg of the horse or pony between the cannon bone and the pastern.

flake — A section of hay that is taken from a bale for feeding, usually about six inches wide and two feet square. There are usually about ten flakes of hay in a whole bale.

flaxen — A cream-colored mane and tail sometimes found on chestnut horses and always found on palominos. If a chestnut has a flaxen mane and tail, he is known as a "flaxen chestnut."

foal — A young, unweaned horse or pony of either gender. When the horse or pony is weaned or separated from its mother, it is called a "weanling."

founder — A painful disease of the foot that may be caused by the overeating of grass or grain when the digestive system of the horse or pony is not used to it. This may cause the tissues and blood vessels inside the hoof to be permanently damaged.

gallop — A fast, four-beat gait where all four of the horse's feet strike the ground separately.

garner — To acquire by effort.

giving the horse his head — Allowing the horse or pony to stretch his neck and feel his way along rather than keeping a tight rein on him.

grain — Harvested cereals or other edible seeds, including oats, corn, wheat, and barley. Horses and ponies often eat a mixture of grains, vitamins, minerals, and molasses called "sweet feed."

gray — A common color found in horses and ponies. A gray horse is born black and gradually lightens with age from a steel-gray color to almost white.

graze — The act of eating grass. Horses and

ponies will graze continually when turned out on good pasture.

groom — To groom a horse is to clean and brush his coat, comb his mane and tail, and pick the dirt from his hooves. A person known as a "groom" goes along on a horse show or horse race to help with grooming, tacking up, or anything else that needs to be done.

halter — Also known as a "head collar," a halter is made of rope, leather, or nylon and is placed on the head of the horse and used for leading or tying him. The halter has no bit, but it has a metal ring that rests under the chin of the horse or pony to which you can attach a lead rope.

hard brush — A grooming tool used on a horse or pony. A brush, resembling a scrub brush, usually with firm bristles made of nylon used to brush dried mud or dirt from the coat and legs.

haunches — Another term for the hindquarters of a horse or pony.

hay — Grass or other herbage that is cut in the field and allowed to dry over several days. It is then usually baled and stored in a barn to be used as feed for animals.

hay net — A nylon or rope net, which is stuffed with loose hay and tied at the top and then hung in a stall or trailer to allow the animal to eat from it.

hindquarters — The rear of the horse or pony, including the back legs.

hitch up — Attaching a horse or pony to a cart, carriage, or sleigh through the use of harness straps.

hoof pick — The grooming tool used to clean the dirt and gravel from the hooves of a horse or pony.

hooves — The hard covering of the foot of a horse or pony. The hooves must be cleaned before and after riding and trimmed every six weeks (or so) to keep them from growing too long.

in hand — Refers to horses shown in halter classes, not mounted.

lead rope — A length of cotton or nylon rope of about six feet with a snap attached to the end. The rope is used to lead the horse or pony when clipped to the halter.

lead shank — Same as a lead rope, but it is more often made of leather with a section near the snap made of chain.

leather conditioner — An oily or creamy substance that is rubbed into leather to help keep it from drying out and cracking.

leg up — The action of helping someone

mount by grasping their bended left knee and hoisting them up and onto the back of a horse or pony.

liniment — A liquid solution rubbed onto sore muscles to relieve pain.

lipped — to touch or feel with the lips.

loft — The large, open area in the top of a barn used to store bales of hay and straw.

longe — A flexible, thirty-foot long rein with a snap on the end used in schooling, breaking, or training the horse or pony.

longe whip — a long whip used along with the longe line to encourage the horse or pony to move in a circle.

mane — The long hair that grows on the crest (top) of a horse or pony's neck and hangs over on one side or the other.

mane and tail comb — Any of a variety of metal or plastic combs used to comb the mane and tail of the horse or pony.

mare — A female horse or pony three years of age or older.

mare's tails — Also known as cirrus clouds, these are wispy cloud formations that actually look like the long, flowing tail of a horse or pony.

milkers — The equipment that is attached to the cow's teats in order to draw the milk out of the udder through a pulsing action.

milk house — The small building attached to a dairy barn where the milk ends up in a cooling tank.

muzzle — The lower end of the nose of a horse or pony, which includes the nostrils, lips, and chin.

neat's-foot oil — A type of oil used to condition leather to keep it from drying out and cracking.

nicker — A low, quiet sound made by a horse or pony in greeting or when wanting to be fed.

paddock — A fenced area, smaller than a field, used for enclosing animals for limited exercise.

pastern — The lower part of the leg of the horse or pony below the fetlock and above the hoof.

piebald — A horse or pony of a black coat color with white patches or markings on various parts of the body.

pinto — A horse or pony of a solid coat color with white patches or markings on various parts of the body. The mane and tail may be various colors.

pony — A pony measures below 14.3 hands from the bottom of the hoof to the withers (see definition). A hand equals four inches — 14.3 hands and above is considered a horse.

progeny — The offspring or descendants of one or both parents.

pulling comb — A small, metal, short-toothed comb used to thin or shorten the hairs of the mane.

quarter horse — A strong, stocky, but gentle breed of horse whose name is derived from its speed at the quarter-mile race. This breed is very popular with cow ropers and western riders.

rail — The term used in riding lessons and horse shows to describe the fencing enclosing the riding ring. To be "on the rail" is to be riding closely to the ring fence. Spectators standing outside the ring are said to be "at the rail."

reins — The leather straps of the bridle attached to the bit and held by the rider to guide and control the horse.

ringmaster — The person at a horse show who assists the judge in the ring and helps any rider who falls; also may replace rails that may be knocked from a jump by a horse.

saddle — A saddle is placed on a horse or pony's back, secured by a girth, and is a leather, padded seat for the rider; part of a harness that is placed on the horse or pony's back behind the withers.

saddlebags — Two leather pouches attached to each other by a wide piece of leather that drapes over the saddle or withers of the horse;

sometimes it is placed behind the saddle to allow the rider to carry supplies on the trail.

saddle rack — A metal or wooden frame attached to the wall or stall on which to hang the saddle.

saddle soap — A creamy soap in a can used to soften and clean leather. The soap is rubbed into the leather and then buffed with a cloth.

salt block — A square, compact brick made of salt and placed in the field or stall, which the horse licks in order to provide him with salt and other minerals.

scrubby mitt — A rubber mitt with short bristles on one side that fits over the hand and is used to bathe the horse or pony.

singeing pan — A low-sided pan containing a small amount of burning lighter fluid that produces a small flame. When passed briefly over this flame, the hair-like under feathers of poultry are removed.

sire — The father of a horse or pony.

skewbald — A horse or pony with a coat color other than black combined with white patches or markings on various parts of the body.

sleigh — A horse-drawn vehicle that does not have wheels but runners for gliding over snow or ice.

slip knot — A type of knot, also known as a "quick release," which can be quickly and easily untied in case of a problem, such as the horse or pony falling down or getting hung up.

soft brush — A brush made for grooming a horse or pony's coat and face; it is the same shape as a scrub brush, but it has softer, longer bristles.

spook — An action of the horse or pony in which they shy away nervously from something they are not familiar with.

springtooth harrow — A piece of farm machinery with curved teeth used to dig furrows into the ground for planting.

square up — A horse or pony is said to be "standing square" or "squared up" when all four legs are placed evenly on the ground, the two front lined up so that no one foot is in front of or behind the other, and hind feet the same. This is the desirable position when showing the animal at halter.

stallion — A male horse or pony that has not been neutered and may be used for reproductive purposes.

star — Any white mark on the forehead of a horse or pony located above a (imaginary) line running from eye to eye.

straw — The material used for bedding in a stall; it consists of the stalks of grain from which the grain has been removed and the stalks baled. It should be bright yellow and not dusty.

sweat scraper — A tool made of plastic or metal that is held in the hand and used to remove excess sweat from a hot horse or pony or excess water from one being bathed.

tack — Equipment used in riding and driving horses or ponies, such as saddles, bridles, harnesses, etc.

tack box — A container with a handle used to transport grooming tools, bridle, and other equipment to horse shows or other events.

tack trunk — A large trunk usually kept in the stable that contains the equipment used by the rider, such as bridles, grooming tools, the saddle, lead ropes, medicines, etc.

throatlatch — The narrow strap of the bridle, which goes under the horse's throat and is used to secure the bridle to the head.

trot — A rapid, two-beat gait in which the front foot and the opposite hind foot take off at the same time and strike the ground simultaneously.

trough — A long, shallow receptacle used for feeding or watering animals.

udder — The mammary glands of a cow where the four teats are attached and the milk is produced.

wash stall — An enclosed area, usually inside the stable, with hot and cold running water where a horse or pony may be crosstied and bathed.

weanling — A foal who has been weaned (separated) from its mother and is no longer nursing. Foals are normally weaned at about six months of age.

whinny — A high-pitched, loud call of a horse.

winter coat — The longish hair that a horse or pony naturally grows in the winter to protect him from the cold. In the spring, the winter coat "sheds out" and the body becomes sleek again with a short hair coat.

withers — The ridge at the base of the neck and between the shoulders of a horse or pony. The saddle sits on the horse's back behind the withers, and a horse or pony's height is measured from the ground to the top of the withers.

Tailwinds Farm

Visitors can relax in country comfort at our lovingly restored Victorian farmhouse — a bed & breakfast which has been featured in *The New York Times*, the *Baltimore Sun*, and on *Good Morning America*.

Conveniently located between Philadelphia, Baltimore, and Washington, D.C., the rolling hills of northeast Maryland beckon horse lovers of all ages to come and enjoy a wide variety of activities — guided trail rides through Fair Hill state park, pony rides for the little ones, carriage rides, riding lessons, summer camp, horse shows, and even special holiday events!

To learn more about the bed & breakfast and stables at Tailwinds Farm, visit our website at www.fairwindsstables.com or call us at 410-658-8187.

JoAnn Dawson with Painted Warrior

About the Author

A horse lover since childhood, JoAnn S. Dawson lives with her husband and two sons on a horse farm and bed & breakfast in Maryland where they offer riding lessons, trail rides, and a summer camp. Her film credits include principal actor in *The Sixth Sense* and *12 Monkeys*, and horse wrangler on Oprah Winfrey's *Beloved*.

JoAnn is the Director of the Equine Institute at a local college and enjoys competing with her horse, Painted Warrior.

Are you a fan of the

Lucky Foot Stable

Series?

Get a signed PHOTO of the author with her horse, Painted Warrior!

... when you join The Lucky Foot Stable Fan Club.

Here's your chance to keep up on the latest news and merchandise, chat with other fans, and have the opportunity to visit Tailwinds Farm, home and riding stable of JoAnn S. Dawson.

Become a member now!
Go to www.luckyfootseries.com

Happy Reading and Riding!